Guns in the Graveyard

The cold air knifed into his lungs as the young lawman gasped for breath in his all-out run. Reaching the cemetery, Buck Durand threaded his way among the tombstones, slipping periodically on the icy snow covering the ground, and as he approached the mausoleum, he could determine by the crack of yellow light showing at the bottom and along the edge of the door that it was slightly ajar. The light also meant that his quarry was inside.

When he inched closer, he could hear the killer talking softly to someone. Taking a deep breath, Buck drew his gun, cocked it, and steeled himself. Then he raised his foot, kicked the door open, and plunged inside. The killer whirled toward him . . .

The Badge Series
Ask your bookseller for the books you have missed

THE BADGE: BOOK 20

★

WIDOW VALLEY

★

Bill Reno

 Created by the producers of
The Holts: An American Dynasty,
Stagecoach, and **White Indian.**

Book Creations Inc., Canaan, NY • Lyle Kenyon Engel, Founder

BANTAM BOOKS
NEW YORK • TORONTO • LONDON • SYDNEY • AUCKLAND

WIDOW VALLEY

*A Bantam Book / published by arrangement with
Book Creations, Inc.*

Bantam edition / December 1990

*Produced by Book Creations, Inc.
Lyle Kenyon Engel, Founder*

ISBN 0-553-28791-5

Published simultaneously in the United States and Canada

Bantam Books are published by Bantam Books, a division of Bantam
Doubleday Dell Publishing Group, Inc. Its trademark, consisting of
the words "Bantam Books" and the portrayal of a rooster, is
Registered in U.S. Patent and Trademark Office and in other
countries. Marca Registrada. Bantam Books, 666 Fifth Avenue,
New York, New York 10103.

PRINTED IN THE UNITED STATES OF AMERICA

OPM   0 9 8 7 6 5 4 3 2 1

WIDOW
VALLEY

★ BADGE ★

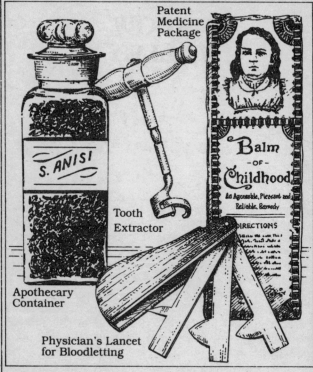

Patent
Medicine
Package

S. ANISI

Balm
— OF —
Childhood
An Agreeable, Pleasant and
Reliable Remedy

DIRECTIONS

Tooth
Extractor

Apothecary
Container

Physician's Lancet
for Bloodletting

A small-town physician of the 1890s was often expected to serve as dentist and pharmacist, even treating animals on occasion, and he frequently made house calls with only the contents of his saddlebags to assist him. Most doctors were familiar with the use of antiseptics, thanks to Lord Lister's discovery about thirty years earlier that wounds treated with carbolic acid did not become infected. For anesthesia, chloroform was available to relieve the agony of surgery; however, most doctors and patients preferred to rely on whiskey as the painkiller of choice.

❈ BADGE 20: WIDOW VALLEY ❈

Chapter One

The cool wind whipping across the rolling hills of southern Wyoming made the long tawny grass look like a storm-tossed sea, and the nip in the air that first week of October 1890 presaged an early winter. With the mid-morning sun on their backs, two riders headed due west. The small man on the rear horse was hunched in the saddle, and his craggy, bearded face was sullen as he rode staring forlornly down at the handcuffs that chafed his wrists. The wind periodically plucked at his hat brim and blew his long, straggly hair in front of his eyes, but he ignored it.

Keeping his prisoner's horse in tow with a lead rope looped over his saddle horn, the big, broad-shouldered man in front kept his head slightly bent into the wind so that his dark-brown, wide-brimmed Stetson obscured his face. Tied on his right thigh, just below the fringe of his tan leather jacket, was a holster bearing a Colt .45, and pinned on his chest was a shield declaring him to be a United States marshal.

Tug Farrell was a formidable figure, especially on horseback, for he was well over six feet and very muscular, and in spite of his fifty years and the slight paunch that was developing at his belt line, he was clearly not a man to tangle with. Dark skinned and having prominent cheekbones —legacies from his mother, who was half Ute Indian— Farrell's handsome face was deeply lined and weathered, but he still attracted the eyes of the ladies. His thick head of curly hair was almost totally silver as was his heavy mustache, but the brows above his penetrating eyes were still quite dark.

Suddenly the lawman pulled rein at the crest of a gentle rise, and the prisoner lifted his drooping head. Rawlins lay sprawled before them, and the guard tower of the Wyoming State Prison loomed against the sky on the west side of town.

The federal man's badge glinted with sunlight as he twisted around in the saddle and looked at the outlaw's sallow face, which now seemed paler as he stared at the gloomy edifice. "Well, Foutz," Farrell declared, "there's your new home."

Bernard Foutz did not respond.

The marshal nudged his mount forward and headed down the slope toward the town. After passing through town, to the stares of passersby, the riders hauled up at the prison gate, and an armed guard stepped out of the tower's cubicle onto a narrow catwalk and looked down at them.

"United States Marshal Tug Farrell," announced the man in the lead. "I'm delivering Bernard Foutz. Warden Childers is expecting us."

The guard called out an order to men on the ground, and the gate swung open. The riders were then ushered across a dismal dirt yard to a wing attached to the fortresslike gray stone main building. Foutz remained in the saddle while Farrell dismounted stiffly and waited for a guard to fetch the warden. Within moments, Warden Ed Childers, a man of sixty, appeared. Looking harried and distracted, the warden extended his hand toward the lawman, saying, "Hello, Marshal Farrell. It's been a long time."

"Guess it has," agreed the marshal while shaking the warden's hand. "At least three years." Indicating the outlaw, he added somewhat unnecessarily, "He's your man."

Childers ordered the guards to take the prisoner, and after the marshal had removed Foutz's handcuffs and the outlaw was led away, the warden stepped past Farrell and suggested, "Come on into my office. Are you hungry?"

"Not yet," replied Farrell, following Childers through the door. "I had breakfast on the trail. But I sure could use a cup of hot coffee."

The warden called for a guard to bring coffee, then closed the door and rounded his desk. He stood for a moment, eyeing the towering figure, then gestured toward a straight-backed chair in front of the desk. "Have a seat."

Farrell sat and pushed his Stetson to the back of his head, asking, "Is something wrong?"

Childers sat down, nodded, and replied, "More than wrong. Potentially horrible. We had a prison break just about an hour ago, and— You ever hear of Swede Andgren?"

"What man in my business *hasn't* heard of him? Are you telling me you had him here and he escaped?"

Childers scrubbed a palm across his face. "That's exactly what I'm telling you."

"I'd heard that the murderous swine had finally been caught."

"Yeah, a couple of months ago. Andgren and his bloody gang robbed the bank up at Lander, killing two citizens during the robbery, and Fremont County Sheriff Bob Stenner immediately formed a posse and gave chase. When they caught up to the gang, Andgren wasn't with them, and after a shoot-out that cost several of the gang— including Andgren's young nephew—their lives, Stenner learned that the Swede had fled alone in another direction. The posse caught up with Andgren and cornered him in the Wind River mountains, and he gave up." Childers opened a humidor and extended it toward Farrell, asking,

"Cigar?" The big man refused with a shake of his head, but the warden took one for himself and lit it.

"So what was Andgren doing here in the State Prison?" queried the lawman. "The man's a cold-blooded murderer. Why wasn't he hanged in Lander?"

Childers had started to answer when a knock sounded at the door, and then a guard entered the office bearing a steaming coffeepot and two cups on a wooden tray. He set down the tray and quickly exited, and when the warden and the lawman were alone again, Childers puffed on his cigar and leaned back in his chair. "As I was about to say, the reason why Andgren wasn't hanged is because of this newfangled approach from back East that's creeping into our law enforcement system."

"I take it you're referring to this 'let them live awhile before we execute them' stuff," Farrell responded, scowling slightly.

"Yep. A year ago Andgren would have been hanged within a day or two after the circuit judge sentenced him to death. But this is 1890, and seeing as how we're living in more enlightened times, instead of being hanged immediately, Andgren was sent down here to stink up one of our cells for a few weeks before taking the plunge. He was to have been hanged next Tuesday."

Farrell took a sip of coffee, then asked, "How'd the Swede make the break?"

"Andgren apparently contacted friends on the outside and set things up. This morning he complained of stomach pains, and while he was in the infirmary getting medical attention, five of his cronies broke him out, taking two guards as hostages before escaping. What guards I could spare are at this moment giving chase."

"You have any idea where he'll head?"

"I know exactly where he'll go. You see, when Andgren was captured and put into jail along with the survivors of his gang, his men told him that his nephew had thrown down his gun and tried to surrender but that Sheriff

Stenner and his possemen cut the youth down in cold blood. The story was complete rubbish, and Stenner flatly denied it, but of course the Swede chose to believe his men and swore he'd break out of prison before he was hanged to kill the sheriff and every member of the posse."

"So he's headed for Lander," mused Farrell.

"No doubt about it," the warden concurred wearily. "And if my guards don't catch him, he'll not only go after Stenner and the possemen, but he'll shed blood wherever he goes. He's like a mad dog."

"How many guards did you send after him?"

"Four. As I said, that's all I could spare. With two guards taken as hostages, I was cutting our ranks mighty thin by sending four more to chase Andgren and his five pals."

"If they're unsuccessful, you'd best wire Stenner and warn him Andgren's headed his way."

"I will definitely do that," the warden assured him.

Farrell and Childers conversed for another half hour and then were interrupted by a loud, rapid knock at the door. Childers called out, "Come in!"

The door opened and a guard entered, his face white. Standing, the warden hurried around the desk and asked, "Clarence, what happened? Did you and the others catch up with Andgren?"

Rubbing the back of his neck with a shaky hand, Clarence Short replied, "We caught up to them, sir, and shot it out with them. We killed one of the gang and wounded another—but we paid a heavy price. Benchley and Roberts are dead, and Griffith took a slug in the leg."

Childers punched his fist into his palm. Fixing Short with anxious eyes, he asked, "You're telling me that Andgren and the others got away, and they still have my men as hostages?"

"Yes, sir. They took their wounded man, along with Cox and Turner, and headed in a beeline for Lander. I couldn't go after them all by myself, and besides, I couldn't run off and leave Jack. He was bleeding bad. I had to get him back here before—"

Raising a hand, Childers cut in, "I wouldn't expect you to go after an armed gang by yourself. You did the right thing by bringing Griffith back." After sending the harried guard to his quarters to rest, the warden turned to Farrell and declared, "I've got to send a wire to Sheriff Stenner immediately! If he and those possemen aren't warned, they're dead."

Deeply concerned about the situation, U.S. Marshal Tug Farrell rode into town with the warden. Entering the Western Union office, Childers dictated a message to the telegrapher. Putting down his pencil, the elderly man shoved back the green visor on his head and hurried with the yellow piece of paper to the telegraph key.

He tapped out the Morse code message, then looked at both men and said, "Should get an answer back shortly. I'll have an acknowledgment within a minute or two from the operator in Lander, and then he'll take the message to Sheriff Stenner. Unless Stenner's out of town or somethin', we'll be hearin' from him right soon."

When three minutes had passed, the old man scratched his bald head and looked at the telegraph key as if it were a sick animal. "Come on," he ordered in a half-whisper. "Start clickin'."

After another minute the telegrapher gazed back at the warden, who stood beside Farrell at the counter, and announced, "Guess I'd better try again."

The old man carefully tapped the message out once more. When there was no acknowledgment after another five minutes, he repeated the message a third time. Still there was no reply. Rising from the chair and returning to the counter, he said, "Gentlemen, this can mean only one thing. There's a break in the wire somewhere."

Farrell's face stiffened. "Andgren! He's cut the wire so Stenner can't be warned!"

"I'm afraid that's it," Childers agreed glumly, nodding.

"Must be," put in the old man. "I got a message from Lander just yesterday afternoon."

"Harvey, how long will it take to find the cut and repair it?" asked Childers.

"Could take a week or so," the telegrapher replied, "since the repair crew has to come out of Laramie City. If the wire's been cut in a lot of places, it could take longer than that."

"Then there's only one thing to do," Farrell stated, picking up the pencil and a sheet of yellow paper. "I'm heading for Lander myself. If I can't stop Andgren and his bunch, I'll ride around them and warn Stenner."

The lawman quickly wrote out a message to the chief U.S. marshal in Denver, explaining the situation and informing him that he was going after Andgren. Since Denver was southeast of Rawlins—the opposite direction from Lander—Farrell assumed that the outlaws had not cut the wire running that way. He was right. The telegrapher sent the wire and received an acknowledgment, and Farrell then told him, "I want you to keep trying to get the message through to Sheriff Stenner, just in case it's only a temporary interruption rather than a break. Can't weather conditions or roosting birds sometimes interrupt service for a while?"

"I guess it's possible, Marshal," replied the old man, "but my experience tells me the line's down. I'll sure keep peckin' at it, though. In the meantime I'll wire Laramie City for help. Could be there's a crew somewhere close, so maybe we can get it fixed real soon."

Farrell and Childers went outside and the marshal mounted his horse. "I'll do my best to come back with Andgren," the lawman promised. "It may have to be with him draped over his saddle, but I'm going to give it all I've got to stop him from doing any killing in Lander."

"I hate to see you go up against so many men alone," Childers said, shaking his head. "Since they've got a wounded man along, they'll probably be moving a bit

7

slow, so if you can go on around them and get to Lander before them, with help from Stenner and some townsmen maybe you can get the jump on those murderous scum and even save the lives of my two guards."

"I'll see how it goes," Farrell remarked as his horse danced about as if sensing that a good run was coming. "If I don't want to ride this animal to death, it'll take me several days to cover the hundred and thirty miles to Lander. You'll hear from me or see me as soon as it's possible." With that, the big lawman spurred his horse and galloped out of Rawlins, heading northwest.

The cold air stung his face as the animal beneath him found a steady rhythm and quickly covered ground. Farrell followed the telegraph line as closely as possible for the first few miles, and soon his suspicions were confirmed: The wire had been cut in numerous places. Swede Andgren meant business; he was clearly bent on killing Sheriff Bob Stenner and the possemen who he believed had murdered his nephew—and he would not allow them to be warned.

The federal lawman rode for quite some time at breakneck speed before slowing his mount to a trot to let the gelding catch its breath. Horse and rider had crossed a creek and were climbing out of a draw when Farrell spotted what appeared to be two bodies sprawled on the ground about a quarter mile ahead. A chill slithered down his spine as he feared the worst, and moments later he slid from the saddle and stood over the two uniformed guards. Both men had been shot between the eyes. Swede Andgren had shown them no mercy.

Link Dunning waited in thick brush on a hilltop with his horse tied in a gully below. The sinewy outlaw's tobacco-stained mouth broke into a smile when he saw the familiar group of horses galloping in his direction, but as the men drew closer his smile faded. Dunning could now see that two of the men were riding double, and there was no question that the man behind the saddle clinging to the other was wounded.

As the thundering horses drew near, Dunning stood up and waved his hat to catch the riders' attention. When they veered his way, he pointed toward the gully behind the hill and ran down to meet them. He reached the bottom of the gully at the same time his cohorts rode in on their gasping mounts.

Cliff Graves had two bullets in his midsection and was bleeding profusely. Dunning stepped close as a couple of the men slid from their saddles and began helping Graves off the horse.

Dunning gave the wounded man a concerned glance, then shook Swede Andgren's hand. "Sure am glad to see you, Swede! We couldn't let you hang."

Nodding emphatically, the big Swede declared, "I appreciate that more'n you could ever know!"

As the others laid their wounded friend on the ground, Dunning asked, "What happened?"

"The guards came after us," Andgren replied. "We took two of 'em as hostages, but four more ran us down and started shootin'. They killed Benny and put a couple of slugs in Cliff. We shot down three of the four and took off. A couple of miles up the road we shot the hostages and left 'em for buzzard bait."

A beefy man standing six feet tall, Andgren ran his stubby fingers through his straw-colored hair as he looked down at Graves. His pale blue eyes regarded Dunning warmly as he said, "You did a good job on the telegraph wire, just like I asked. Looked to me like you cut it in at least a dozen places."

"More like two dozen," Dunning corrected, laughing. "It'll take 'em more'n a week to get it back in service."

A wicked leer etched itself on the Swede's broad face. "I'll have Stenner and his posse taken care of before then."

The outlaw tending the wounded man poured water

9

from his canteen into his cohort's mouth. Graves took a few swallows, and then he looked up at Andgren with bleary eyes and said weakly, "Swede, I can't ride no more."

"You've got to," countered Andgren, his strong will evident in his voice, allowing for no argument. "We have to keep movin'."

Graves said no more. After a brief rest for the horses, the outlaws were in the saddle again, galloping toward Lander, and Cliff Graves once again held on to his friend's waist.

As darkness began falling, the outlaws neared a clump of trees some distance away from a cluster of ranch buildings. Graves called painfully to Andgren, saying, "Swede, I can't ride no farther! Please, let's camp for the night in those trees!"

Andgren slowed the group to a walk and shook his head, replying, "I was plannin' on ridin' till about midnight. We can't stop yet. Besides, those trees ain't far from that ranch house over there."

One of the other men suggested, "Them cowboys ain't gonna know we're here if we're quiet and don't build a fire, Swede. Cliff's about done in. He's got to have some rest."

"Okay," Andgren resignedly agreed. "We'll make a cold camp and hole up in the trees. But since that bunkhouse over there is mighty close, we gotta keep our voices low—and let's hope the horses don't nicker and give us away."

The crescent moon soon rose in the clear sky, casting its pale light through the trees that had already shed a goodly amount of their leaves. Two of the outlaws worked on the wounded man in the dappled moonlight, doing what they could to stop the bleeding. When they had made him as comfortable as possible, they joined the others sitting around on the ground, eating cold beans and hardtack.

As Graves's two cohorts opened their bean cans, Andgren asked them softly, "What do you think, fellas? Is he gonna make it?"

"He's in bad shape," one of them replied. "If we don't get him to a doctor real soon, he's gonna die."

The Swede thought a minute, then suggested, "Maybe we oughtta take him close to that bunkhouse and leave him for the hands to find. They'd no doubt get him to a doctor."

"Yeah, and to a lawman, too," spoke up Dunning. "I think we oughtta take him to a doctor ourselves."

When the others chorused their agreement, Andgren pondered the idea for several minutes, then said, "Tell you what, boys. Why don't we just split up in the mornin'? I'm right obliged to you for bustin' me outta that stinkin' prison, but I can handle what's got to be done alone. In fact, that's the way I'd prefer it anyway, since I want to do all the killin' myself. After all, it was *my* nephew those skunks murdered. I want to sneak in there and kill that sheriff and those possemen one at a time, makin' the others sweat good while I'm killin' their pals off slow-like."

"You're sure that's the way you want it?" Dunning asked.

"Yeah. You guys get Cliff to a doc as quick as you can—the nearest town without backtrackin' to Rawlins is probably Creston—and I'll get my revenge on Stenner and his bunch and meet you somewhere in a couple of weeks. We'll work together again if you want and start cleanin' us out some more banks."

"Sounds good to me," one of the men, Jake Tibbs, announced, getting up. "You guys pursue that line of thinkin' while I take a trip a little farther into the trees. Be back in a few minutes."

Fifty yards from where the outlaws were scheming together, U.S. Marshal Tug Farrell dismounted and ground-tied his horse, having easily followed the gang's trail as they held a straight line toward Lander. Opening his

11

saddlebag, the lawman took out his extra revolver and checked the loads, then snapped it shut. He slipped the other gun from its holster, cocked both Colt .45s, and then crept slowly toward the clump of trees. As he did so, he could see lights in the windows of the ranch buildings on the other side of the woods.

Farrell listened to the outlaws' low voices as he moved closer, glad that the moonlight was bright enough to allow him to pick his way stealthily. Drawing up behind a tree, he assessed the five men huddled near each other, four seated and one lying close by, and he was certain that they were Swede Andgren and his remaining gang members and not just some cowhands or drifters. Then he heard the big Swede comment that he had to steal some clothes somewhere and get out of the prison grays, and his certainty was confirmed.

The lawman abruptly rounded the tree, wielding two guns, and bellowed, "Get those hands in the air! I'm United States Marshal Tug Farrell, and you're all under arrest!"

Startled by the towering, menacing figure illuminated by the moonlight, the outlaws complied.

"Now, you boys are going to shed your weapons one at a time," the marshal ordered. Glaring at Link Dunning, he barked, "You first! Reach down real careful and lift that revolver out of the holster with your fingertips, then toss it gently at my feet. One quick move and the coyotes will eat your body tomorrow."

In the trees to Farrell's right, Tibbs was returning to the others when he heard the lawman's booming voice. Stopping short, he swore under his breath, drew his gun, and cocked the hammer, then shifted direction so as to get behind the marshal.

Link Dunning slowly reached toward his holstered gun while keeping the other hand lifted high. He glanced furtively at Andgren, who met his gaze but kept a stolid expression on his face.

12

The marshal then looked at Andgren and blared, "You next, Swede!"

Suddenly a twig snapped behind Farrell, and he instinctively leapt sideways, pivoting at the same time. Tibbs's gun roared, but the bullet missed its target, and the lawman fired at the flash. Tibbs wailed as he went down and lived only a few seconds longer.

At the same time, the three outlaws who still had their guns pulled them, while Dunning dived for the revolver that he had thrown at Farrell's feet. The sudden eruption of gunfire made the coppice sound like a battlefield as the seasoned lawman hit the ground rolling to evade the hot lead.

Farrell's weapons boomed in return as he made himself a moving target. One of the outlaws took a slug in the throat and collapsed, making a sickening, gurgling sound. Another rose to his feet, gun blazing, and was hit by a bullet in the chest. Andgren blasted away at the dark, evasive form on the ground, but he took a slug in his right thigh and dropped to the hard earth, losing his weapon in the process.

Dunning's gun slipped from his fingers when he first attempted to pick it up, and by the time he finally gripped it solidly and aimed it at Farrell, the marshal was turning from Andgren and lining his right-hand Colt on him. Dunning fired, striking the marshal in the left upper arm, but as Farrell was hit, his aimed revolver fired a slug into Dunning's heart.

The bullet's sudden impact slammed Farrell to the ground, his revolvers falling from his hands. He could hear Swede Andgren cursing and trying to find his gun, but beyond him were distant, excited voices that were growing ever louder.

Andgren cursed as he groped for his revolver. Finally his fingers curled around the butt of his gun, and he rose unsteadily to his feet. Limping toward the lawman, the gang leader panted, his breath hissing through his teeth as he raised his gun to shoot Farrell.

The shouts of the ranch hands racing across the field distracted the killer. Squinting in their direction, he could see that they were drawing close. By the time he turned back to Farrell, the lawman was reaching for his own revolver.

Time was of the essence to Andgren. Holstering the gun, he limped to his horse, cursing his pain, and hauled himself into the saddle. He quickly glanced back at the bodies of his friends before gouging his horse's flank with his good leg. As he galloped away, Farrell fired at his back, but the bullet thwacked into a tree. Then the ranch hands closed in and surrounded the lawman with their guns drawn, demanding to know what was going on, as Swede Andgren fled into the night.

Chapter Two

A few miles south of Lander, rancher Vic Hoffman was whistling a tune as he left his barn carrying a bucket of milk toward the back door of the house. The air was crisp, and fog lifted off the surface of the Little Popo Agie River as the Wyoming sun came up, throwing long shadows across the valley.

Feeling the bite in the air, the lanky thirty-year-old gazed to the east at the brilliant yellow leaves on the aspen trees that covered the hills. Overhead, a V-shaped formation of ducks winged its way southward. *It's the second week of October*, the rancher reminded himself. *Old man winter will soon be here.*

As he reached the house the rancher glanced at the Wind River Range to the west. The rising sun was lighting up the magnificent mountains, setting their jagged peaks afire. Hoffman loved this beautiful valley and every day was happier that he had decided seven years ago to make his home here. Just before stepping onto the porch he glanced expectantly at the road to the north, but seeing no movement he continued on.

The hinges on the kitchen door squeaked as he entered, and he reminded himself for the hundredth time that he needed to oil them. But the reminder was quickly forgotten when he smelled the frying bacon and hot coffee. Walking to a small table where a milk strainer sat atop another bucket, the rancher poured the milk into the strainer and glanced at his wife, who was occupied at the stove and had her back to him.

"The chores are all done, honey," he told her. "There's no sign of the Stenners yet, but they ought to be pulling in any minute. Breakfast about ready?"

Emmy Hoffman, who was two years younger than her husband but looked barely over twenty, turned around and smiled. Her light-brown hair cascaded in soft swirls to her shoulders, and a stubborn wisp lay on her forehead. "Just about," she replied in a cheerful voice as she brushed back the lock of hair, "so I hope something hasn't detained our illustrious sheriff. You go ahead and wash up."

Setting the empty milk bucket on the floor, Hoffman took off his hat, exposing his curly, carrot-red hair. He tossed the Stetson expertly onto a wall peg ten feet away, then removed his blue denim jacket and hung it next to the hat. Stepping behind his slender wife, he put his arms around her, kissing the back of her neck. Emmy giggled like a schoolgirl and pivoted around inside his arms. They kissed tenderly, and he asked softly, "Why do I have to wash up?"

Emmy giggled again. "Because your hands smell like a cow's udder. Now, quit acting like your son and get your hands washed."

Hoffman walked over to the washbasin, noting that Emmy had set only four places at the table. Picking up a bar of lye soap, he plunged his hands into the hot water that his wife had already poured for him and asked, "Aren't the kids going to eat breakfast with us?"

"They're still asleep," Emmy responded. "I'll feed them later."

Nodding absently, Hoffman looked out the window

toward the road. There was still no sign of the Stenners. "I don't see them yet, honey," he murmured.

Emmy was placing a sizzling skillet into the overhead oven to keep it warm. Closing the oven door, she queried, "You *did* tell Bob and Corrie to come for breakfast, didn't you?"

"I sure did. But I really didn't have to, since they always eat breakfast here when Bob and I go deer hunting—which I don't need to remind *you* we've been doing since we moved here."

"And you *did* tell them seven o'clock?"

"Yes, ma'am, but that really wasn't necessary, either, since they've also known for years what time we eat breakfast. I'm sure they'll be here soon." Grinning in a mock-snide way, he added, "Are you and Corrie going to sit around and gossip all day, or are you going to do something useful?"

Emmy gasped playfully and threw a dish towel at him. As he caught it in midair, she laughed and said, "I don't like such an insinuation, mister smart aleck! For your information, we plan to sew."

Chuckling, Hoffman remarked, "Well, you can still gossip while you sew."

Her hands on her hips, she countered, "Tell you what, my dear, we'll probably spend the whole day gossiping about our husbands!" Then her tone grew more serious and she said, "I'm glad you and Bob are such good friends, because I certainly do enjoy Corrie's company."

The minutes passed, and Emmy tried to keep breakfast from burning yet from getting cold. At seven-twenty the lanky redheaded rancher looked again at the road, but the Stenners were still not in sight. Just as Emmy suggested that they should go ahead and start or the food would be inedible, they heard a horse snort outside. Shoving back his chair, Hoffman declared, "They're here," and he dashed to the back door to meet them.

Stepping onto the porch, the rancher was surprised to

see Deputy Sheriff Buck Durand dismounting. The young sandy-haired lawman was alone.

"Morning, Buck," the redhead said. "Didn't expect to see you today."

At twenty-three, Buck Durand was tall, sinewy, and ruggedly handsome. Stroking his well-trimmed mustache, Buck's blue eyes twinkled expectantly as he explained, "I'm your hunting partner for today."

Emmy came through the door as Hoffman frowned and asked, "Is something wrong with Bob?"

"No," Buck replied quickly, touching his hat brim politely as he nodded at Emmy. "It's Mrs. Stenner. She came down with a high fever last night. Dr. Bristol is with her, but Sheriff Stenner wants to stay close. He asked me to ride out and tell you why they couldn't make it—and he also said I should take his place on the hunt."

Concerned, Emmy asked, "Will Corrie be all right?"

The deputy nodded. "Doc Bristol told the sheriff he didn't think it was serious, ma'am. He thinks she'll be okay in a day or two."

"Well, I'm relieved to hear it." Looking up at the tall young man, Emmy queried, "Have you had breakfast?"

"Ah, no, I haven't, ma'am. The sheriff told me you'd eat at seven, but I had a few things to take care of before taking off, so I'm a bit late. If there's any food left, I wouldn't mind at all having some."

"There's plenty," she assured him, smiling. "And I suggest we get inside and eat it before it gets cold."

Going inside, Buck took off his hat and placed it on the back of an unoccupied chair and then dug in, wolfing down the delicious food. Emmy was a bit pensive while the two men discussed the hunt, with Buck mentioning he had a new high-powered rifle he was eager to break in, and he was excited about sharing the day with Hoffman. He was sure he would get himself a healthy supply of venison before sundown.

After a few minutes Hoffman noticed Emmy's mood and said, "What's wrong, honey?"

Dabbing listlessly at her food, the pretty woman answered, "I'm concerned about Corrie. She's my very best friend, and I sure don't want anything to happen to her. She's— Oh, what am I fretting about?" she suddenly chided herself. "With Doc Bristol looking after her, she's in good hands."

"I'll agree with that, ma'am," confirmed the deputy after swallowing a mouthful of food. "The doc knows his stuff—from delivering babies to broken bones and from breaking fevers to digging out bullets, he's the best there is."

"We sure think the world of him," Emmy agreed. "He's pulled our children through some real tough sicknesses. I guess there isn't a soul in this valley who doesn't love him. The man's a godsend." After a slight pause she said, "It's just too bad a man still so young is a widower. He needs a wife."

Buck chuckled. "Well, from what I've observed, ma'am, there are quite a few unattached women around who have ideas along that line."

"I can believe that," Emmy responded with a laugh. "If Doc were ten years older, I'd play Cupid and try to get him and Beth Farnham together."

"Well," interjected Buck, "aside from their age difference, I wouldn't wish Mrs. Farnham's troubles on Doc. She's certainly got her hands full with Ron."

Emmy nodded. "You're right. Too bad Ron isn't like the other two boys."

Conversation faded, and everyone focused on his food. A few minutes later Hoffman laid his knife and fork on his plate and asked, "Well, Deputy Durand, are you about ready to go? If we don't get after that big buck deer you've got your heart set on, he'll die of old age before we find him."

Emmy cleaned up the kitchen while her husband and the young lawman went to the barn to saddle Hoffman's horse and bridle the pack mule. When the men returned to the back porch, she stepped outside, wiping her hands on a dish towel, and asked, "How long do you two plan to stay out?"

Hoffman chuckled. "Till we get our deer or the sun goes down—whichever happens first."

"Which way are you going?"

Hoffman had his Remington bolt action 30.06 in hand. Shoving it into the saddleboot, he answered, "We'll ride west past Beth Farnham's place and head in the general direction of Fremont's Peak. Once we're at a higher level in the timber, we'll work our way south."

After kissing his wife, the rancher mounted up and said, "Sorry about Corrie. I know you two always have such a good time."

"There'll be other times," Emmy stated with a resigned shrug.

The men rode out leading the pack mule and eager to get into the hunt. The long sweeping valley surrounded them, magnificent in the early-morning sun, while directly ahead some ten or so miles lay the foothills of the Wind River mountains with the snowcapped peaks behind them.

Gazing at the sight, Vic Hoffman mused, "It sure is an incredible place to live. I'm glad my children were lucky enough to be born in such a breathtaking and peaceful place."

Soon they drew abreast of the Farnham ranch and saw the three Farnham sons in a nearby field. Hank and Willie, who were seventeen and fifteen respectively, were standing on a haystack—the last cutting of the season—pitching the hay onto a flatbed wagon, while twenty-two-year-old Ron stood on the wagon and caught the animal fodder. Spotting the rancher and the deputy, the two younger boys smiled and waved. Hoffman and Buck waved back. Seeing his brothers waving, the older Farnham turned to see who was passing by, and when he recognized the two men, he scowled.

Ron's head whipped around toward his brothers, and the two riders could hear his sharp voice, though they were too far away to hear the words clearly.

Without looking back, Hoffman commented, "Ron's a surly cuss, isn't he?"

"That's putting it mildly," said Buck. "He's got a hair-trigger temper and he's meaner'n a snake."

"I've heard about him starting fights in town," remarked the redheaded Hoffman.

"All the time. It's been that way since he was nine or ten years old. He was always the big troublemaker in school. Thinks he's pretty tough."

Hoffman chuckled. "From what I hear, he *is* pretty tough."

"Well, I guess so. By the time Ron turned fifteen, even Fred Farnham couldn't handle him anymore. My father and Fred were close friends, and he used to come over to our place and tell Dad some of the awful things Ron had done. Just plain mean, that's what he is. He was bad enough before Fred died last year, but since then he's gotten worse. He thinks he owns that ranch all by himself, and he's rough with his mother and beats his brothers."

"Maybe he ought to be behind bars."

"Maybe—except he's never broken any laws. There's nothing on the books that says you can be jailed for being mean to your mother and beating up your brothers. Bad as he is, Ron's never stepped outside the law."

"Funny that he seems to have a bit of community spirit," Hoffman remarked. "At least he's ridden with us every time we've had to have a posse."

"I don't know if it's community spirit or just that he volunteers to ride in the posses so he can show how tough he is," Buck remarked with a derisive sniff.

Hoffman sighed. "Too bad Beth Farnham's stuck with

21

a handful of trouble when instead Ron ought to be a help to her. She and my wife are pretty close friends, and Beth has shared some of her heartaches with Emmy."

"Your wife has a sweet way about her, Vic," the deputy allowed. "I'm glad Beth has her to talk to."

The rancher smiled. "Yep, Emmy's a wonderful woman, all right—and I'm a mighty lucky man."

Soon the Farnham property was out of sight and the two men were nearing the foothills. Hoffman gazed up at the higher elevations and declared, "There's a big ol' buck deer up there just waiting for us, my friend. I can feel it in my bones."

"I sure hope that feeling in your bones means I'll soon be tasting one of his steaks in my mouth!" Buck said with a laugh.

At the haystack Ron Farnham glared at his younger brothers and rasped, "Get back to pitchin' that hay! We don't have time to lollygag, wavin' at people!"

Willie looked at his big brother askance and said, "I think it's only right to be friendly with our neighbor . . . and it sure doesn't hurt to be nice to the law. You ought to get to know Buck Durand better. He's really—"

"Nobody's tellin' you to think, kid!" Ron spat, cutting off Willie's words. "Now, get to pitchin' hay!"

Sticking up for his sibling, Hank bristled. His face flushed as he said sharply, "You've got no call to treat Willie like that! Nobody made you boss of this place when Pa died!"

Ron swore loudly at the middle brother and jabbed the air with his finger, snarling, "Somebody had to take charge, so I did it! If you think you're big enough to be boss, just hop to it!"

Though he was almost as big as Ron, Hank was not as strong or as fast with his fists. Keeping his voice level so as not to provoke his brother any further, he said, "I don't hanker to be nobody's boss, but I still say you've got no call to treat Willie mean for wantin' to be friendly."

"What you say doesn't cut no ice with me, Hank," Ron snapped. "Get back to work."

Hank and Willie exchanged a look of disgust and Ron saw it. Temper flaring, he jumped to the ground from the wagon, glared at his brothers, and yelled, "Get down here, both of you!"

Hank and Willie looked at each other again, fear on their faces. Eyeing Ron, Hank protested, "You're gettin' mad over nothin'. You want to get this hay in the barn, right? So let's do it."

Ron was livid with fury. "I said get down here! If I have to come up and get you, it'll go twice as bad!"

Both teenagers reluctantly jammed their pitchforks into the haystack and slid off the stack. As Hank reached the ground, his older brother met him by slapping him viciously across the mouth. When the youth rebounded off the haystack, Ron slapped him again. Enraged, Ron then turned to a frightened Willie and buffeted him with a series of stinging backhanded blows. When the youngster tried to cover his face with his hands, Ron batted them away and slapped him harder.

His rage finally spent, Ron took a couple of steps back, glowering at the boys with piercing eyes, and snarled, "Now, get back up there and pitch hay!"

The brothers climbed back to the top of the stack, their faces red and smarting, and once again pitched hay to Ron on the wagon. As soon as the wagon was loaded, the elder Farnham drove it to the barn and parked it directly beneath the hayloft door. While his brothers climbed onto the hay in the wagon, Ron entered the barn and scurried up the ladder to the loft, then pushed the double doors open wide.

Sullen and clearly resentful, Hank and Willie began pitching hay to Ron from the wagon. The older youth grew increasingly irritated by their demeanor, especially

Willie's. Badgering the youngster, Ron demanded, "Hurry up, Willie! You're not pullin' your weight! Come on! Snap to it down there!"

Suddenly Willie Farnham had had enough. He threw his pitchfork to the ground, fixed Ron with a hard glare, and shouted, "If the way I'm doin' it ain't good enough, do it yourself!"

The wagon jerked as Ron leapt down from the loft door onto the vehicle, fire in his eyes. Before either Willie or Hank could react, their older brother seized the boy by the shirt and threw him off the wagon, and Willie struck the ground, rolling, with Ron right behind him. Hank jumped off the wagon, shouting at Ron not to hurt Willie, but the older youth's rage was in control, not his sense. He pulled his little brother to his feet, then knocked him flat with a stiff punch to the jaw.

Hank drew up beside Ron and said, "That's enough! Leave him alone!"

Without warning, the older brother punched Hank on the temple, knocking him down. Willie was rising to his feet and weeping as Ron pivoted and charged after him. In desperation, Willie swung a fist at his brother's face, but Ron grabbed the arm in midswing, spun Willie around, and slammed his head against a corner of the wagon. The boy howled and tried to fight back, but his resistance infuriated Ron all the more, and Ron repeatedly banged Willie's head against the wagon until the boy sagged and fell to the ground, unconscious.

That was all that Hank could stand. He leapt onto Ron's back, and the brothers went down together, threshing and grunting as they wrestled. Ron pounded Hank's face several times, but Hank was finally able to get loose and rise to his feet.

Furious at the assault, Ron tackled Hank, and they rolled precariously close to the wagon team. The frightened horses whinnied and danced nervously, and Ron tried to wrestle his middle brother into the hooves so the horses would step on him. But Hank was strong enough to prevent that, and he broke free and got up. Ron went after him, ducking a blow, and knocked him down.

Just as Hank was gamely getting up again, Beth Farnham rounded the barn from the house side, having heard the ruckus. When she saw Willie on the ground with blood running across his face and Ron about to administer further punishment to Hank, she dashed in, screaming, "Ron! Stop it! Leave him alone!"

Ron smashed a fist against Hank's mouth, knocking him against the wagon, then turned toward his mother, eyes flashing, and shoved her to the ground. The fifty-year-old woman tumbled in the dirt. Hank railed at his brother, stumbling after him as Ron dashed into the barn, but he gave up the chase and turned back. He helped his mother off the ground and hurried with her to Willie.

Kneeling beside the unconscious boy, Beth began to weep as she examined the gash on Willie's forehead. She pulled a handkerchief from her dress pocket and tried to stay the flow of blood, and stroking her son's bruised cheek tenderly, she sobbed, "Willie! Willie, wake up!"

"Ma, he doesn't look so good," Hank whispered hoarsely. "I'd better go after Doc Bristol."

"We've got to bring him around, honey," Beth insisted, her gray-streaked brown hair falling in her face. "Go get some water."

Hank returned with a bucket of water to find his mother still talking to her unconscious son, pleading with him to wake up. Hank was about to pour some water onto Willie's face when the barn door slammed open, and he and his mother looked up to see Ron leading his saddled horse out into the sunlight. After giving them both a poisonous stare, Ron swung into the saddle.

Beth stood up, her whole body trembling. With tears streaming down her face she screamed at Ron, "You wicked devil! You're nothing but a brute beast!"

Ron Farnham spit in the dirt, eyed her malevolently, and galloped away.

Beth's weeping grew louder as she watched her oldest son ride from sight. Her breast heaved as she screamed after him, "Beast! Filthy beast!"

Wiping away her tears, she turned back to Willie, who lay bleeding and still. Hank was splashing the cold water in his brother's face, but there was no reaction. After some ten minutes of trying to bring Willie around, Beth said with quivering lips, "Let's get him in the house. I've got to do what I can to stop the bleeding. You'll have to ride to town and bring Doc Bristol."

Hank carried his unconscious brother to his room and gently laid Willie on the bed, and Beth soon came in, carrying a wooden box containing medical supplies. She had no way to stitch up the gash, but she would clean it and keep a compress on it to slow the bleeding.

Hank stepped back, allowing his mother to sit beside Willie, and said, "I'll get going, Ma. Be back as soon as I can with the doc."

As he started for the door Beth called, "Son?"

Pausing, he looked back. "Yes, Ma?"

"Maybe you'd better bring Sheriff Stenner with you. You know your brother's temper," she murmured, her voice faltering. "He might just get angrier while riding and come back here ready to do us all harm."

Blinking, Hank said shakily, "I hadn't thought of that, Ma, but you're right. I shouldn't even be leavin' you. Ron could come back while I'm gone and—"

"There's no choice, Hank," cut in Beth. "You've got to bring the doctor."

"But if Ron comes back madder'n he was when he left, he might beat you, and I can't let that happen. It's plenty important that Willie has Doc Bristol look after him, but it's just as important that Ron doesn't harm you." After a moment's thought he said, "I know! I'll go after Deputy Durand! He and Vic Hoffman rode by a short time ago, and I could probably catch them faster'n I could get to town for the sheriff."

"Do you know where they were going?"

"It wouldn't take but a few minutes to ride over and ask Emmy. She'll know. I'd feel a lot better while ridin' for Doc if I knew the deputy was here with you. He can handle Ron."

Beth was clearly terrified of her oldest son. "All right," she agreed. "But please hurry. I'm worried about Willie."

Emmy Hoffman was dishing up hot cereal for four-year-old Maggie and six-year-old Bobby when she heard rapid hoofbeats approaching the house. When she reached the door, Hank Farnham was already on the porch.

Seeing the worried look on the youth's face, Emmy asked, "Hank, what's wrong?"

The teenager explained the situation, then asked if she knew where the deputy and her husband had gone.

Nodding, she replied, "Vic told me they would head toward Fremont's Peak, go into the high country, and then head south."

"I'm sure I can catch them before they get that far," Hank said with confidence. "Thanks for your help."

As the youth turned to leave, Emmy touched his arm and said, "I'll tell you what. I'll take Bobby and Maggie and go stay with your mother till you and the deputy get there. Ron wouldn't do anything to us."

Adjusting his hat on his head, Hank replied, "I don't suppose he would, ma'am, but he's awfully unpredictable. When his temper's up, he's dangerous."

"Your mother needs me right now," countered Emmy. "I'll hitch up the wagon while the children are eating their breakfast. We can be there in no time."

Smiling weakly, Hank said, "I really appreciate your willingness to help, Mrs. Hoffman. You're a right good neighbor."

With that, Hank Farnham bounded across the porch

and vaulted into the saddle. His horse kicked up clods of dirt as he put it into a gallop and bolted in the direction the hunters had gone.

Emmy watched him for a moment, then sighed and went back into the kitchen. Looking at her children, she thought to herself, *Poor Beth. She has so many troubles, while I'm so fortunate and have none. It would be downright selfish not to give her support in such a time of need.*

Chapter Three

Vic Hoffman and Buck Durand rode into the low foothills and began a gradual climb among the gold-leafed aspens, heading for the tall timber and high country. A stream gurgled nearby, and the morning breeze carried down the scent of pine from the higher elevations.

They rode in silence for a while, then Buck asked, "You and Sheriff Stenner have hunted these mountains a lot together, haven't you?"

"We sure have," Hoffman replied. "We always have a good time together. Bob's a great guy."

"He's a good man to work for, too," remarked the deputy. "Take today, for example. He's had a day off coming for a long time, while I've gotten them regularly. There's plenty to do back in town, but he knows I like to hunt, so he insisted I go along with you. It's mighty nice of him to let me come."

"Maybe he can come out in a few days, after Corrie's feeling better," the rancher suggested. "I'll make time for him, that's for sure."

"The sheriff told me about the big grizzly that got your dog a couple of years ago."

"Three years, to be exact," Hoffman said wistfully.

"Bob and I thought we had found us a moose, and Shep ran ahead of us as we rode through the timber. When we saw a huge male grizzly loping aways ahead, we just about swallowed our tongues. We knew the movement we had seen through the trees was being made by something large, but we sure didn't know we had a grizzly for company."

"Your dog went after him, did he?"

"Yeah. The bear roared, and I guess old Shep thought he could bark and scare him off. Went charging after him. I tried to call him back, but it didn't do any good. The bear hit him once with his huge paw and ripped him open something awful and broke his back. Bob and I hid till the bear decided to move on, then picked up what was left of Shep and buried him under a pine tree nearby. Emmy was real torn up about it, and she hasn't wanted another dog since."

The men rode on in silence, moving higher. From the corner of his eye, Hoffman appraised Buck from time to time, thinking that he had great admiration for the sandy-haired young lawman. He knew that the deputy's father, Newt Durand, had the largest ranch in the valley—the Box D—and that he was by far the wealthiest rancher in the county. It was common knowledge that Newt had wanted both his sons to stay at the ranch, eventually to become part owners, and that he was furious when Buck sought the job of deputy sheriff and was appointed. He was so angry that he rewrote his will, cutting Buck's portion of the inheritance to only twenty-five percent and leaving the rest to Buck's older brother, Errol. Newt had then rubbed salt in his younger son's wounds by making Errol foreman of the Box D at twice the pay. People in the valley figured such a thing would not have happened if Buck's mother had been alive, but she had died when he was twelve.

Curious about Buck's decision to become a lawman in the face of his father's disapproval, Hoffman broke the silence by saying, "You know, I've always wondered why you gave up the chance to be part owner in your dad's ranch and went against him."

"It's quite simple," the young deputy declared. "Every man knows in his guts that he's cut out to do one main thing in life. And no matter how much money he has, if he's not fulfilling his destiny, he's miserable. I love horses and cattle, and I enjoy working with them, but ever since I was knee-high to a gnat, I've had a burning desire to wear a badge. I was born for law enforcement like you were born to be a rancher."

"I can understand that," said Hoffman. "But still, it took courage to stand up to Newt Durand."

"I won't tell you I didn't have a few sleepless nights before I made my move," Buck stated. "I knew Dad would probably do something rash if I went against his wishes, but I have my own life to live . . . and I want to live it with a badge on my chest."

"It must have hurt, though, when he changed the will, didn't it?"

"Yes, sir, it hurt deep. But if I hadn't followed my guts, I'd have been miserable. I'm plenty happy as deputy sheriff, and someday when I have enough experience under my belt, I'll seek me a sheriff's badge somewhere."

"That's admirable," commented Hoffman. "I hope you're able to realize your dream." He paused, then asked, "Does this situation make it difficult for you when you visit your father's ranch?"

"It's a little sticky, since I'm considered the black sheep of the family," admitted Buck. "There's not a lot that Dad and I can talk about, and Errol hardly speaks to me at all. But I still go out once a week or so. They're the only family I've got, and even though there's a strain, I love them and want to be with them."

The rancher studied the young deputy's face for a moment, then remarked, "I don't mean to stick my nose in where it doesn't belong, but there's talk in the valley that there's bad blood between you and Errol because of Jenny Bristol, and that the two of you are headed for a showdown over her."

The mention of Dr. John Bristol's beautiful daughter brought a smile to Buck's lips. Shifting slightly in the saddle, he looked at the rancher and replied, "It's true that Errol and I are both in love with Jenny. Like just about every other eligible man in town, we fell for her the first time we laid eyes on her when she and Doc came to Lander two years ago. Jenny's weeded her way through a passel of suitors, and during the last few months she's narrowed her beaux down to just Errol and me. But even though we both want her real bad, it's not going to come to anything like a showdown."

"But I've heard Errol talk pretty poorly about you for going against your father's wishes. If Jenny should choose you instead of Errol, isn't he liable to get . . . well, *riled*?"

"He might," the young lawman conceded, "but we're brothers. There won't be any violence between us."

The rancher said no more, and as they rode on, Buck's thoughts returned to the night before, when he and Jenny had been alone, walking in the moonlight. He remembered the sparkle in her dark-brown eyes when she looked at him and whispered, "Buck, I realize now that while I'm fond of Errol, it's you that I love. It's you that I want."

Buck recalled how his heart had thundered in his chest at her words, and he could still taste the sweetness of the kiss that sealed the bond of love between them.

Jenny had explained that Errol had asked her to the dance at the town hall that night, and she had agreed to go, planning to tell him afterward that it was Buck she loved. "I know it will be hard for him," the young woman had mused, "but I'm sure Errol will soon forget me and look elsewhere for the woman destined to be his for life."

Vic Hoffman broke into Buck's thoughts, saying, "We're far enough into the tall timber, my friend. Let's leave the horses in that ravine where they'll be sheltered from the wind and start hunting."

Riding down into the ravine, they skirted the large jagged boulders and thick patches of brush. A small stream ran across the bottom of the ravine, and somewhere out of sight they could hear the water falling from a precipice to some spot lower down the mountain.

The air was thinner and colder at the higher altitude, and both men buttoned up their jackets and turned up their collars. Moments later, wearing sidearms and carrying high-powered rifles, the hunters excitedly climbed out of the ravine and headed for higher ground. Barely ten minutes had passed when the deputy spotted a huge buck deer standing amid a stand of pines sixty yards ahead. He touched Vic Hoffman's arm and pointed, and they both froze in their tracks. The wind was coming from in front of them, preventing their scent from reaching the deer.

As each man moved cautiously behind a pine tree Hoffman whispered, "You spotted him, Buck. Take your shot!"

The magnificent animal took a few steps, sniffed the wind, and unwittingly gave the deputy a clear shot by moving into a small clearing. Holding his breath, Buck braced the rifle against the tree, sighted in, and squeezed the trigger. The rifle boomed and the buck jerked as the slug ripped into his breast a little left from center. Grunting, he fell flat on his belly and rolled onto his side.

"I got him, Vic!" the young lawman shouted.

"Beautiful shot," the rancher declared. "Let's go."

They approached the deer with caution, for there was a chance he was still alive and could be on his feet and charge if he was only stunned. But he was dead, the high-powered slug having exploded his heart.

Buck was excitedly examining the huge antlers, saying that he would hang them in the den of his house, when the rancher pointed down the steep slope and said, "We've got company."

The lone rider was weaving his horse rapidly among the trees, and when he got closer, they saw that it was Hank Farnham. The youth waved at them, though the look on his face told them something was amiss.

Drawing up, Hank reined in his mount and said breathlessly, "I saw your horses down below. The gunshot helped me find you."

"What's wrong?" queried Hoffman.

Young Farnham described the trouble at the barn and how his brother had ridden off in anger, leaving Willie unconscious. "I'm afraid Ron'll come back more dangerous than he was when he left and will hurt Ma while I go get Doc Bristol. I'd appreciate it if you'll protect her, Buck."

"We'll both come, Hank," Hoffman offered.

Laying a hand on the rancher's arm, Buck insisted, "There's no need for that. I'm the law, and it's my responsibility. Besides, I can handle Ron myself."

"Okay, then I'll dress out your deer," Hoffman insisted.

Nodding his thanks, Buck took Hank's offered hand to ride double down to his own mount and climbed up behind him, settling onto the horse's rump. He then told the rancher, "See you later."

Hoffman nodded back. "See you later."

Hank and the deputy trotted off and soon disappeared from sight. Rifle in hand, the rancher made his way down to the ravine. By the time he reached his horse, it was standing alone, and he shoved the rifle into the saddleboot and then removed the block and tackle from the pack mule's back, along with a lariat. He led the mule back up the steep slope to the buck, and using the lariat as a tow rope, he tied the dead deer behind the mule and dragged the heavy carcass back down to the ravine. After stringing up the buck by its heels to an overhanging limb with the block and tackle, Vic removed his long-bladed hunting knife from his saddlebag and went to work.

It was early afternoon when Vic Hoffman finished

dressing out the deer, and he carried the knife to the small stream running through the ravine where he washed the blood off his hands and the knife in the ice-cold water. Returning to the carcass, he was about to lower it onto the pack mule when his horse and the mule began nickering nervously. Both animals began dancing about, tugging at the reins tying them fast to the limbs of large bushes.

Hoffman knew they smelled something, and he made a slow panorama but saw nothing. The animals settled down, and the rancher hoped that whatever was in the area had moved on. Just as he was about to release the tension on the rope, the horse and mule bobbed their heads and snorted, once again pulling at the reins. Suddenly the redhead saw movement at the crest of the ravine, but whatever it was quickly disappeared. Keeping his eyes pinned to the ridge, he talked to the animals in a soothing voice, trying to calm them, but their eyes were wide with fear. His heart began to pound as he pulled the rifle from its boot, then once more looked around.

There was movement again at the rim of the ravine, and this time Hoffman was able to make out a gray ball of fur. Abruptly another flashed by. Wolves! The scent of fresh blood had undoubtedly drawn them.

Hurrying up the steep grade, he jacked a cartridge into the chamber of the rifle, holding it ready to fire. As he neared the top he saw four wolves slink into the brush, the last one pausing to look at him.

Hoffman knew that wolves naturally feared man and would not attack a human unless they were rabid, starving, or cornered. They were definitely not cornered, the chance that they were starving was remote, and the chance that they were rabid was even more remote. He figured a rifle shot would be enough to scare them off now that they had seen him, for it was the dead deer they were after, not him.

Aiming the rifle above the spot where he had seen the wolves vanish into the brush, he fired a shot. For good measure, he worked the lever and fired a second time, then wheeled and ran back down into the ravine. Replacing the rifle in the saddleboot, he led the mule beside the swaying carcass, and gripping the antlers, he hoisted the head and neck onto the mule's back. The mule snorted, showing its disfavor for the dead thing touching it.

Steadying the pack animal, Hoffman put his shoulder underneath the shoulder of the deer and worked the dead weight farther onto the mule's back. When he was satisfied that the carcass would be balanced once it was lowered, he began to work the pulley, easing the deer down.

The mule bobbed its head and grunted. "Easy, boy," the rancher said quietly. "This ol' deer's dead. He isn't going to bother you."

The mule showed its teeth, snorted, and let out a high, shrill sound. This time Hoffman knew it was not the weight or the smell of the deer that was bothering the mule, for his horse whinnied with definite fear and began dancing about, pulling at the reins.

Breathing an oath, he mumbled, "So those pesky wolves have come back in spite of the rifle shots, eh?"

He looked around, trying to spot them, but they were staying out of sight. Grumbling to himself, he wondered if he was going to have to put up with scaring off the wolves all the way down the mountain.

The horse's eyes were wild. It fought the reins that held it to the tree, bending the branch to the breaking point. Hoffman decided he would get his rifle and fire off a few more rounds, but first he would have to finish lowering the deer to the mule's back and get it balanced. He was struggling against the mule's nervous movements when the branch holding his horse's reins snapped, and the terrified animal galloped away down the steep slope, the broken branch flying in the air on the end of the reins.

"Hey!" he shouted. "Come back here, boy! Those wolves aren't gonna hurt you!"

Muttering curses at the fleeing horse, he returned to

the mule and the deer. His words abruptly died and a sudden chill ran through his entire body as he caught sight of what had terrified his mount. Standing on its hind legs between two pine trees was a massive grizzly bear. Like the wolves, the gigantic beast had caught the scent of fresh blood and had followed it to its source.

Vic Hoffman's mind ran back to the day his dog was killed by a grizzly about the same size as this one, which was a male and stood every bit of nine feet tall. The huge beast cocked its head, eyeing the rancher defiantly, then opened its mouth, displaying enormous sharp teeth. The roar that followed seemed to shake the forest. Behind Hoffman the mule shrieked and galloped away, and the buck fell to the ground, lying with its head twisted beneath its body and the great antlers angling unnaturally.

The terror the rancher was feeling iced his bones and knifed through his intestines. Cold sweat moistened his body as he thought about his rifle carried away on the frightened horse. He was alone, on foot, with only the Colt .44 in his holster, and whether he ran or stood still, the bear would attack him. If he fled, it would draw the beast automatically, and if he remained where he was, it would make him appear as an impediment to the deer.

The grizzly took two steps closer, lifted its head, and emitted another thunderous roar, spraying saliva. Hoffman swallowed with difficulty, thinking, *Maybe if I back away slowly, he'll want the deer bad enough to let me leave*. His knees felt watery as he began moving backward, easing his hand down over the butt of the revolver. He knew the handgun would be little defense against a creature of such size, and he would use it only if the bear charged.

Its brown coat glistening in the afternoon sun, the grizzly watched Hoffman with wary eyes. The terrified man kept his gaze glued to the bear as he inched his way in cautious retreat. Suddenly the grizzly roared again, opening its massive mouth, and at the same time, it swung both front paws, claws distended, as if giving its prey an example of what was about to come. Hoffman sensed in his bones that the beast was going to charge.

Even as he whipped the gun from its holster, the grizzly dropped to all fours and raced toward him. Hoffman's hand trembled as he thumbed back the hammer and fired, and the bullet struck the beast in the left shoulder, causing it to falter. No more than forty feet away now, the bear roared and rose on its hind legs, shaking its ponderous head. Panic gripped the rancher, squeezing his spine with a chilling hand, as the grizzly thundered onward.

Hoffman cocked the gun and fired point-blank at the bear's immense furry chest, hoping to send the slug into its heart. The impact of the slug would have knocked a man down but served only to infuriate the enormous beast. Backtracking quickly, the rancher fired again, putting another .44 slug within an inch of the first one. Then his feet tangled in a tree root, and he fell on his back, catching a glimpse of blood on the bear's left shoulder as it kept coming.

Just before it reached him, Hoffman managed to roll out of reach and gain his feet. Though it must have been feeling the sting of the bullets in its thick body, the grizzly was unhindered in its movements. It lunged for Hoffman, swinging a huge paw, and the rancher shot it again in the chest, hoping the bullet would penetrate the hide and pierce the heart. The bear kept coming. This time he would aim between the eyes.

Gritting his teeth, he raised the muzzle, taking a step back to get a good angle. But he lost his footing on the steep slope, and he tumbled head over heels down the embankment. The revolver discharged harmlessly as it slipped from his fingers on the way down, bouncing and landing on a flat rock.

When he hit the bottom of the ravine, Hoffman collected himself, rolled to his knees, and looked up at the bear. The gigantic beast stood at its full height, roaring and waving its deadly paws. The rancher's head was spinning. He saw the gun lying on the rock fifty feet above him, and he tried to remember if there were any bullets left. How many had he fired? Four? No, five! Or . . . was it six? No, it was five. He was sure of it. One in the shoulder, three in the chest, and one that missed. Five. There was one bullet left. But would it really matter, even if he could get to the gun before the frenzied animal came thundering down the slope? Only if he could put a bullet between its eyes—and that was an awfully big if.

Blood was now bubbling from the three holes in the grizzly's chest. It licked at the wounds, smearing the red liquid over its coat. Its shoulder was spurting blood as well, and it was clear that the pain and confusion the bear was experiencing was making it angrier by the moment. Another roar split the air, and then the beast looked down at its foe.

On his feet now, Hoffman found that there was something wrong with his right knee, which was throbbing painfully. He must have hit it on a rock while tumbling down the slope. Taking his eyes off the bear for a quick look, he saw that his pants were torn at the knee, and there was blood showing at the spot. While the grizzly alternated between licking its wounds and gauging its prey, the rancher looked up at his revolver fifty feet away, its barrel shining in the sun. If he had any chance at all, it lay in the single bullet left in the gun. He had to get to it before the bear came after him. Taking a deep breath, he lunged up the steep embankment, but fiery pain shot from his injury, and the knee seemed to cave in.

The grizzly eyed him furiously and seemed about to charge after him when it suddenly stopped and whipped its head around at the sound of the wolves slashing into the carcass of the deer. The bear bellowed fiercely, pivoted, and went after the wolves.

Hoffman's heart pounded in his chest like a triphammer. The wolves had given him a chance. Steeling himself to ignore his pain, he scrambled toward the gun on the rock. He could hear the wolves answering the growls of the bear with growls of their own. Suddenly there was a sharp yelp, and a wolf came sailing over the edge of the ravine, legs flailing. It struck the ground some ten feet to Hoffman's right and rolled to the bottom of the ravine, its coat ripped open. The creature tried to get up but collapsed on its side and lay there, whimpering. The frightened yelps of the other wolves grew ever softer as they fled.

Forcing himself onward, the rancher continued climbing toward his gun. He was within ten feet of it when he saw the maddened grizzly standing at full height, looking down at him. A fresh wave of terror washed over Hoffman as the giant beast went down on all fours, preparing to lunge. The rancher gritted his teeth, and though the pain from the injured leg was excruciating and each movement was pure agony, he clawed his way toward the revolver. After what seemed hours he was almost within arm's reach of the weapon when the massive grizzly leapt straight at him.

A scream locked in Hoffman's throat as he saw the bloody mountain of fur descending on him, and summoning all of his strength, he jumped to one side. The bear's huge body struck him a glancing blow, sending him reeling to the bottom of the ravine. Man and beast struck level ground almost at the same time.

The breath was knocked out of the rancher, and his whole body was racked with pain. Looking quickly around, he saw the grizzly some ten or twelve feet away, lumbering to its feet. A feeling of utter helplessness washed over Hoffman as the gigantic beast began slowly moving toward him, shaking its head. The three .44-caliber slugs in its chest were beginning to take their toll—but it was not happening fast enough.

Sucking hard for air, the rancher forced himself to stand and make a last-ditch effort for the gun. As he turned to go back up the slope, he saw the revolver lying no more than a dozen feet away. The bear had apparently knocked the weapon down in its leap. Hope rose within Hoffman. The grizzly was weakening and moving slower, and a bullet in the head might finish it off.

Hoffman's knee gave way again as prepared to go after the gun. Falling flat, he looked up to see the frenzied grizzly looming over him, bleeding and roaring with fury. He tried to evade the powerful paws, but suddenly they found their mark. He screamed wildly as the claws ripped through his leather jacket, tearing his flesh and bloodying him. Again and again the grizzly clawed and tore at the man, sending sharp stabs of blinding agony through Hoffman's body. Flesh was torn from the rancher's face as he tried to protect himself, kicking and screaming at the same time. The claws kept coming, slashing and gouging and ripping at him. Vic Hoffman knew he was about to die, for the claws would soon tear the life out of him.

All of a sudden, the grizzly stopped its attack, took two faltering steps back, and fell. The slugs in its chest were finally having an effect. While the bear lay there, grunting and struggling to get up, Hoffman rolled onto his hands and knees. A bloodied mess, his face was on fire and there was blood running into his right eye, but he was alive and in one piece.

But so was the grizzly.

Hoffman began crawling toward the gun. Every move was hellish agony, but the battle would not be over until either he or the beast was dead. It seemed like an eternity of eternities, but finally the cool butt of the revolver was in Hoffman's blood-sticky hand. Rolling onto his back on the sloping ground, the rancher saw the bear straightening on its hind legs, shaking its head. Towering, it came for the kill.

Hoffman had but one chance. Drawing upon every ounce of strength left in him, he rose to his feet. The blood on his hands made it difficult to get the hammer

41

back in firing position, but after three tries, it clicked into place.

The massive animal lumbered at its enemy. As Hoffman raised the Colt .44, his head began to go light. *No!* he screamed at himself. *You will not pass out!*

The bear was almost on him, its head thrown back, mouth open, a roar exploding from deep within its chest. Hoffman squeezed the trigger and felt the gun buck against his palm, but the sharp report of the gun seemed muffled and distant as the rancher collapsed to the ground, unconscious.

Vic Hoffman came to in a hazy, gray world. Blinking to clear his vision, he lay there, trying to collect his thoughts. Where was he? What had happened to him? Then it all came back. With effort he sat up and looked down at himself. There was blood all over the front of him, and his leather jacket was in shreds. His knee felt as though a red-hot iron had been laid against it, and the right side of his face was burning as if it were on fire. Blood was clotted in the corner of his right eye.

The empty revolver lay beside him, and a few feet in front of him lay the massive grizzly. It was dead.

It took Hoffman several minutes to get to his feet, for his strength was almost gone. Examining the grizzly, he saw that the last shot he had fired had sent the bullet through the beast's mouth and into its brain. Stumbling toward the stream, he dropped to all fours and shrugged off the shredded jacket. He then took off his shirt, which was torn up as bad as the jacket, revealing his chest, which was a mass of blood. Easing himself over the bank, he stepped into the shallow stream and lay in the water.

Though it initially stung painfully, the cold water stimulated and revived him, and after soaking for a full ten minutes, he wrapped himself with what was left of his shirt to try to stay the flow of blood on his chest and then put the jacket back on. The claw marks on his face were already clotting.

Once again on his feet, the wounded rancher knew he had to find his horse. Maybe it had not run too far. Straining every muscle and limping as he went, he followed the stream southward as his horse had done when it galloped away.

The sun was beginning to set as Hoffman staggered from tree to tree down the mountain. While leaning against an aspen to catch his breath, he looked ahead at a broad meadow and saw the horse and the pack mule standing together, nibbling contentedly at the brown grass. Both animals nickered as he struggled toward them.

After falling twice he finally reached them. It took him several minutes to work his way into the saddle, but when he was finally mounted, he leaned against the saddle horn, patted the horse's neck, and gasped, "Take me home, boy."

Chapter Four

Bobby and Maggie Hoffman were playing in a back room of the Farnham home, and lacking adult understanding, they did not feel the heartache filling the big ranch house. Beth Farnham was on the edge of hysteria as she sat beside her son Willie's bed, looking down at the still-unconscious boy. The frantic woman held his hands as Emmy Hoffman stood behind her, gripping her shoulders reassuringly. Tears stained Beth's cheeks and her lips trembled as she asked, "Emmy, why did this awful thing have to happen?"

Shaking her head, Emmy replied softly, "I'm no sage with great wisdom. I can only say that things happen to us that we cannot explain or understand."

Drawing a shuddering breath, the Farnham woman murmured, "What have I done to bring such terrible things down on me? Ron has always given me so much heartache, and then Fred had to die, leaving me not only a widow but having to handle Ron alone. And now Willie may die. Oh, Emmy, why am I being punished like this?"

The younger woman squeezed Beth's shoulders and answered, "Honey, what's happened to you isn't punishment. You've been a good wife and mother all these years, and you mustn't torture yourself thinking these heartaches are because of something bad you've done. Life is just made this way. For some unknown reason, some people seem to face more tragedies than others. Please, don't blame yourself. And don't give up hope for Willie. His breathing is steady, and Doc Bristol will be here soon."

"I'm so frightened," said Beth, sniffing. "Ron is like a crazy man when he's angry. You . . . you shouldn't be here, Emmy. Please, take the children and go home. I love you for what you're doing, but if Ron comes through that door madder than he was when he left, you and the children could get hurt—or worse."

Emmy knelt down beside her friend and looked her in the eye. "Beth, there's no way I will leave you. If Ron comes home still angry, we'll handle the situation at that time."

"But—"

"No buts. I could never face myself again if I left you."

Beth released Willie's limp hand, took a handkerchief from a nearby bedstand, and blew her nose. Then, dabbing tears from her cheeks, she whimpered, "What's taking Hank and Doc so long?"

Still on her knees, Emmy gripped one of Beth's hands and said, "It hasn't been that long since Hank left my place, and remember, he had to find Vic and Buck before he headed for town. But he's certainly found them by now and is no doubt on his way to town, and my husband and the deputy are probably riding here at this very moment. Once they arrive, we won't have to fear Ron."

Clutching the handkerchief, Beth held it to her quivering lips and, her voice a mere squeak, lamented, "Oh, Emmy, what will they do to Ron if Willie dies?"

"Let's not think in those terms. Let's believe Willie is going to be all right. We have to—"

"Hello!" a male voice suddenly announced from the

front of the house. "Mrs. Farnham, it's Buck Durand! Are you here?"

Beth mumbled, "Oh, thank God!" as Emmy jumped to her feet and dashed from the room.

"We're back here, Buck!" Emmy responded, running along the hallway.

They met just as she reached the parlor, looking past the deputy for a familiar face.

"How's Willie, ma'am?" asked Buck.

"He's still unconscious," Emmy replied sadly, taking another look toward the door. "Is Vic with you?"

"No. We shot a deer just before Hank found us, and since I figured I could handle Ron if need be, he stayed to dress out the deer and bring it off the mountain. Has Ron showed up?"

"No."

"Good. Doc and Hank ought to be here in another hour or so—that is, if Hank finds him in town. Is Mrs. Farnham with Willie?"

"Yes," responded Emmy, turning back toward the hall. "Come. She'll be relieved to see you."

Fremont County's deputy sheriff had been at the Farnham ranch nearly two hours when hoofbeats sounded from the yard. Buck jumped up from his chair and headed toward the door, and Emmy started to follow, but the young lawman waved a hand at her, insisting, "You just stay comfortable, ma'am. This'll be Doc and Hank. I'll bring them in."

When the deputy reached the front door of the house, Hank Farnham and Dr. John Bristol were dismounting. Buck stepped out on the porch and eyed the man he planned to make his father-in-law.

The handsome Bristol was a very young forty-three. His coal-black hair and mustache showed no gray, and his muscular body was still trim. As Buck looked into the physician's warm dark-brown eyes, he understood why so many of the unattached women in the valley had *their* eyes on him.

The doctor untied the black leather bag attached to his saddle horn and turned around, saying, "Howdy, Buck. Is Willie conscious yet?"

"No, sir," replied the deputy. Keeping his voice low, he added, "Frankly, he looks pretty bad."

"How's Ma holdin' up?" queried Hank as he moved toward the porch.

"Not too good," came Buck's quick reply. "Fortunately Ron hasn't come back."

"Is Mrs. Hoffman here?"

"Yeah. She's been a real help to your ma."

"Bless her," Hank breathed, opening the door to let the doctor through.

Bristol paused in the parlor, waiting for directions. After the deputy stepped inside, Hank brushed past the doctor, saying, "This way."

When they reached the door of Willie's room, Hank gestured for Bristol to enter, then followed with Buck on his heels. Emmy Hoffman rose from her chair, as did Beth Farnham, and the harried woman reached for Hank but kept her eyes on the doctor as her son took her in his arms.

Bristol stepped beside the bed, studying the unconscious youth. He lifted the moist cloth that covered the gash on Willie's forehead, examined the wound closely, then dropped the cloth back in place.

When the physician merely stood silently looking at Willie, Beth gasped, "You've got to do something, Doctor! You *can* help him, can't you?"

Bristol set his bag on the bedstand and looked into the desperate mother's eyes with compassion. "I'll do everything that's in my power, Mrs. Farnham," he responded softly.

As the doctor turned back to Willie, Beth kissed her

middle son's cheek and said, "You're a good boy, Hank. You're a good boy."

Hank continued to hold her close.

Bristol pulled a stethoscope from his black bag and clipped it around his neck, then sat on the edge of the bed. As he prepared to listen to Willie's heartbeat, Buck inquired, "How's Mrs. Stenner?"

"Her fever's about the same," responded Bristol as he thumbed Willie's eyelids back and examined his eyes. "I left her in Jenny's care." He smiled proudly, adding, "Though my beautiful daughter hasn't had any formal medical training, she's learned a great deal from her father, and she'll take good care of the sheriff's wife."

The doctor checked Willie's pulse with his fingertips, then opened his shirt and listened to his heart. Hank helped his mother back onto her chair and knelt beside her, holding her hand as she kept her eyes glued to the physician.

Worry showed on Doc Bristol's face as he felt the boy's forehead and carefully checked Willie's pupils. Finally, Bristol looked at the anxious mother and sighed. "Beth, I'm afraid Willie is in bad shape."

Beth's hand went to her mouth. Her face was ashen and her voice was unsteady as she asked, "How bad?"

"He definitely has a severe concussion and . . . well, there may be brain damage."

The tormented woman screamed with agony, oblivious of the attempts by Hank and Emmy to comfort her. "Oh, my poor little Willie! My sweet baby!" she shouted over and over.

She continued wailing and sobbing, and the physician instructed Emmy and Hank, "Let's get her to her bed, and I'll administer a sedative to calm her down."

Hank half-carried his mother to her room down the hall and laid her on the bed. Bristol dissolved the sedative powders in a glass of water and made Beth drink it, then spoke to her quietly. "I've got to stitch up the gash on

Willie's forehead. Emmy will stay right here with you. See if you can't get a little rest, okay? I'll be back shortly."

Hank followed Bristol back into Willie's room, where the deputy sheriff was waiting. While the physician cleaned the wound and prepared to sew it up, Hank stood near and asked, "Doc, is there a chance Willie won't make it? I mean, that he'll die?"

Bristol paused, looked over his shoulder, and replied, "Unfortunately, yes. You see, I have no way of knowing the extent of the damage to his brain." He shook his head, muttering, "Ron must have slammed his head against that wagon awfully hard."

Hank shook his head. "Ron's as strong as a bull when he's mad, sir." His brow furrowed and he said shakily, "If Willie dies, Ron'll face murder charges. They'll hang him."

Buck stepped beside the youth and said, "They won't hang him, Hank. If your brother dies, the charge will be manslaughter, not murder, because Ron didn't intend to kill Willie. He'd go to prison for a long time, but he won't be hanged."

The teenager's face crumpled and tears welled up in his eyes. Weeping, he said, "It can't happen! It just can't happen! Ron deserves to be punished, but if he goes to prison, it'll destroy Ma. I mean, on top of havin' to bury Willie, I don't think she could take the shame of Ron goin' to prison."

The physician started to say something but held his tongue and turned back to his patient.

After a long moment Buck suggested, "Why don't you and I leave Doc to do his work. Let's go outside and take a walk. I think a little fresh air would do us both good about now."

Hank agreed, and they left the house after advising Emmy they would be close by. After busying themselves outside for almost an hour, they returned to the house. Hank stepped into his mother's room to check on her, finding Emmy seated at the window and Beth on the bed asleep.

When Emmy saw the youth, she tiptoed across the room to him and whispered, "She's sleeping peacefully. My children are doing fine by themselves, so I'll stay here to be with your ma when she wakes up."

"I don't know how to thank you, Mrs. Hoffman. It's awfully nice of you to do this."

Emmy smiled. "Giving comfort and being there when you're needed is what friendship is all about. Besides, it gives me a good feeling."

Hank started to reply when Buck whispered his name from the hall. He and Emmy turned and saw Dr. Bristol standing by the doorway. The physician's face was drawn and pale, and Hank's heart leapt to his throat. Emmy glanced at the sleeping woman and followed Hank into the hall, closing the door behind her.

Doc Bristol's eyes were sorrowful as he looked at Hank and said, "Willie's dead, Hank. I'm sorry. I did everything I could."

Hank Farnham's eyes reflected his pain, and his face stiffened and lost color, making him suddenly look much older than seventeen. Emmy gathered him in her arms and led him to the parlor while the physician and the deputy followed.

"What about Mrs. Farnham, Doctor?" asked Buck. "Should we wake her?"

"Let's not," responded Bristol. "The sedative will wear off soon enough, and no doubt once she learns that her son's dead, she won't sleep for quite some time."

While Emmy comforted Hank, the men stepped out on the porch. Sighing, Buck stated, "Ron will have to be brought in, so it looks like the sheriff and I will have to go on a manhunt."

Bristol glanced at the setting sun and remarked, "You may not have to. He'll probably come riding home at sundown since he doesn't know he's in trouble."

Rubbing his chin, the deputy said, "Yeah. You're right. Chances are he'll ride right into my hands. I'll just stay here till—"

Hank Farnham's voice rang out from inside the house, declaring, "Ma, you should still be lyin' down!"

Bolting into the house, the deputy and the physician found Beth Farnham leaning against the wall where the hallway met the parlor. Hank and Emmy were flanking her, their faces filled with worry.

"I looked in Willie's bedroom, but he's sleeping," Beth stated. Seeing Bristol come through the door, she asked, "How is Willie doing, Doctor?"

The physician stepped to her and took hold of an arm. Ushering her toward the sofa in the parlor, he said, "Let's get you off your feet, Beth."

As the older woman sat down, she studied the faces of those who stood before her and squinted, then stated anxiously, "Something's wrong. Did Ron come back? Did he cause more trouble?"

Bristol looked at Hank, gauging if the youth wanted him to break the sad news. Hank's mouth tightened, but his eyes told the doctor that he would do it.

Kneeling down in front of his mother, he gripped her hands and said, "Ma, Willie isn't asleep. He's gone, Ma. Willie died."

A sorrowful howl echoed through the house as Beth Farnham cried out for her young son. It was several minutes before she calmed down somewhat, and when she had settled into quiet weeping, Emmy Hoffman suggested, "Doctor, I'm sure you need to get back and see your other patients, but if you leave some sedative powders, I'll administer them to Beth as you direct. I'm going to stay here with her and Hank."

As Bristol nodded, Hank asked, "What about your husband, ma'am? Won't he be worried when he gets home and you and the kids are gone?"

"He'll figure out where we are, since he already

knows there's trouble here," answered the lovely young woman.

"I'm staying, too," spoke up the deputy. "Doc and I figure Ron will be showing up here about sundown, and I've got to arrest him and take him in."

Hearing the young lawman's words, Beth cried out again, and it took her son some time to soothe her.

Bristol went to Willie's bedroom, covered the body, and picked up his bag. After giving Emmy several packets of powders, explaining the dosage, he closed his bag and said, "You're right, I do need to get to town and see to Corrie Stenner. I'll come back in the morning to check on Beth."

The sun was touching the mountain peaks as Dr. John Bristol mounted his horse and rode toward Lander.

At the Box D ranch, roughly five miles northeast of the Farnham place, Ron Farnham sat in the den of his only friend, fifty-two-year-old Newt Durand. Ever since Ron's father had died, he had turned to the wealthy rancher for counsel, and the rancher sincerely tried to help the young man bring his temper under control.

The diminishing rays of the sun came through the windows of the elegantly furnished room as the two men sat in plush chairs, facing each other. Looking down on the men from the walls and over the big stone fireplace were the heads of a moose, a buck deer, an antelope, a cougar, and a wolf. In the middle of the highly waxed hardwood floor lay a bearskin rug with the head still attached.

The rancher—built much like his son Buck except for a spreading paunch—chewed on an unlit cigar as he listened to Ron Farnham tell about losing his temper with his brothers and what he had done to Willie. "I don't know why I have such a time holdin' my temper, Mr. Durand. It seems like I get to a certain point and somethin' goes deep red in my mind, and I just want to crush and destroy whoever or whatever is annoyin' me. I realize I was wrong to get mad at my brothers for takin' time to be friendly to Mr. Hoffman and your son. I was just tryin' to keep 'em workin' so they don't go lazy on me. It's a tough job, runnin' the ranch without Pa."

"From what you've told me when we've talked before, son, you've had this problem for a lot of years. Seems to me you're going to have to take a long, hard look at yourself and decide you don't like what you see. You've got to tell that hotheaded part of yourself that some big changes have to be made, and they've got to be made right now. Understand?"

"Yes, sir. You're right," Ron breathed, clearly ashamed.

"What you did to Willie was very serious, but maybe things had to come to this point to get you to see the kind of person you've been."

Shaking his head and looking at the floor, Ron said, "I've been rotten, Mr. Durand, plain rotten. There's been nothin' good in me at all."

"Now, I wouldn't say that," Newt countered mildly. "You've done some good things for the community. How about the times you've volunteered to ride in a posse when Sheriff Stenner needed help? Ever since you reached legal age, he's always been able to count on you. Weren't you in on the posse that caught that murdering Swede Andgren and his bunch?"

"Yes, sir."

"Well, there, you see? Don't get down on yourself too much, son. You're not all bad. You've just got to work on those areas that need working on."

Nodding, the younger man said, "You're right, sir. And I feel so bad about what happened—but I hate the thought of goin' home and facin' my ma and my brothers. It'll be like . . . well, like eatin' dirt."

"Maybe eating a little dirt is what you need, Ron," Newt remarked. "The taste of it might stick in your craw and remind you to keep a cool head next time you start to lose your temper. Don't you think so?"

Ron sighed. "Yes, sir."

"Then the thing for you to do is plant your posterior in your saddle right now and ride for home. Tell your mother and those boys that you've been wrong and ask their forgiveness. I know your mother. She's a fine woman. Hank and Willie are fine boys, too. Show them you're man enough to admit where you've been wrong, and I'm sure they'll forgive you."

Silence prevailed in the room for a few seconds, and then Ron looked directly into his friend's eyes and said, "I don't know, sir. You can't forgive *your* son for becoming a lawman. Why should my mother forgive me?"

Newt's mouth dropped open. He grabbed the cigar to keep it from falling in his lap and retorted, "The difference is Buck has never asked for forgiveness! If he ever walks through that door and tells me he's been wrong and asks me to forgive him, it'll be done quicker'n a salamander's tongue can catch a fly. If the badge comes off and Buck comes back to live at the ranch, I'll rewrite my will to read exactly as it did before."

Ron looked at the floor, pinching the bridge of his nose. He was quiet for a brief moment before looking up and murmuring, "Well, I guess if you could forgive Buck, Ma can forgive me." Rising from the chair, he added, "I'm goin' home, and I'm gonna ask her and my brothers to forgive me."

"Good!" exclaimed the rancher, rising also.

At that moment twenty-five-year-old Errol Durand entered the den, accompanied by his best friend, ranch hand Ford Loker. Tall, muscular, and handsome, Errol had sandy hair and blue eyes just like his father and younger brother, though where they were rangy, he was thicker bodied. He greeted Ron, who was the same age as Loker, then looked at his father, asking, "Am I interrupting something, Pa?"

"No," replied the elder Durand. "Ron and I have been chatting, but we're through now."

"Well, I know you'll want to walk Ron to his horse, so let me ask you something real quick."

"Sure," the rancher responded, nodding and sticking the unlit cigar back in his mouth.

"Ford's been with us for nearly five years, and I think we need to pay him more than he's getting. How about giving him a forty-dollar raise per month in salary?"

The boss of the Box D thought for a moment, then asked, "Is this request based on the fact you two are such good friends—or because you honestly can say he's worth another forty a month?"

Gazing levelly at his father, Errol replied, "I'm not interceding on Ford's behalf as his friend. I'm here as foreman of the Box D. You can take my word for it. He's worth another forty dollars."

"Then he's got it," Newt promised, grinning.

Loker, who was blond, lean, and very tall, thanked both men sincerely and left.

Errol watched him go, then turned to his father. "I'm going into town shortly. Anything I can get you?"

"Can't think of anything," Newt responded, scratching his gray-streaked hair. "But isn't it sort of late to be going to town now? It'll shortly be sundown."

"Your memory is slipping, Pa," the younger Durand replied, laughing. "I told you last week that I was taking Jenny to the dance at the town hall tonight."

Newt chuckled. "Oh, yeah! So you did."

"Thought I'd leave right away so I can be there plenty early."

"Can't blame you," said Newt. "That Jenny is one gorgeous young lady. If I was in your boots, I'd want to get there early, too."

Ron Farnham sighed and remarked, "You're one lucky guy, Errol. I tried to get Jenny to notice me for a long time, but she acted like I was invisible or somethin'.

Never could get her attention. But tell me, what about the triangle between you and your brother? Where does Buck stand with Jenny now?"

"Triangle?" Errol replied with a chuckle. "It doesn't exist anymore. Buck's all but out of the picture. Jenny loves *me* and plans to become my wife."

Newt's bushy eyebrows arched. Taking the dead cigar from his mouth, he declared, "This is all news to me, son! When did Jenny tell you that it's you she loves . . . and when did she accept your proposal?"

Errol's face tinted. Clearing his throat, he replied, "Well, the truth is she hasn't come right out and said it's me she loves, but lately I can read it in her eyes. After the dance tonight, we're going to take a little moonlight stroll, and when the time is just right, I'm going to pop the question."

"Oh, you are, eh? And you're dead certain she's going to say yes?"

"Dead certain," Errol answered, echoing his father. "My little brother is just going to have to find him another woman."

Errol excused himself and headed for his room, and Newt walked with Ron to the front porch of the huge ranch house and watched him mount up. Smiling, he asked, "How about riding over tomorrow, Ron? I'd like to know how things go with your mother and the boys."

"Sure," young Farnham agreed, smiling back. "Don't know what part of the day it'll be, but I'll do it."

"Good! See you then."

Ron lifted a hand in good-bye and spurred his horse, galloping across the lush Box D property.

The last rays of light fanned out behind the Wind River Range as Ron reached the road that ran by the Hoffman place, where he turned due west. A short while later he saw his own place in the distance, and butterflies flitted about in his stomach. To delay facing his family just a little longer, he slowed the horse to a walk.

As he drew near a stand of cottonwood trees he was unaware that a man holding a cocked revolver was hiding in the shadows. The man waited until Ron drew abreast of the tree before stepping from his cover, his gun pointed at the young man's chest. When Ron saw him and recognized the face, he stiffened in the saddle, with disbelief showing in his eyes. Before he could react, the revolver roared and Ron peeled off the horse's back, hitting the ground hard. He was dead.

Laughing, the killer walked to the body and stood over it. After a few moments he wheeled, hurried into the trees to his horse, and swung into the saddle. He was still laughing as he rode away.

Chapter Five

Bleeding profusely and in severe pain from being mauled by the grizzly, Vic Hoffman hung onto the saddle horn as his horse slowly carried him from the south across the valley toward his ranch. The bear had clawed him deeply on the chest and abdomen, and once he had been out of the cold water of the stream for a while, the wounds had begun to flow again.

A short while before, he had passed out and fallen to the ground, but he had managed to remount despite his weakness and pain. Now, dizzily leaning over his horse's neck, Hoffman saw that the sun was already well behind the mountains. Clinging tenaciously to the saddle horn, the redheaded rancher told himself he could still live through this if he could get home. Emmy would pack his bleeding wounds and send for Doc Bristol.

Suddenly, barely aware of it, he slipped from the saddle again, and the impact of the fall shot pain throughout his body. Crawling with extreme effort to his horse, which had taken a couple of steps after he had fallen, Hoffman reached the animal and tried to stand. But his strength was waning, and he could only lie on his side and touch the stirrup with his right hand.

Gritting his teeth, he stretched with agony and was able to grasp the stirrup firmly. Using his left hand for added strength, he managed to hoist himself high enough to hook his right elbow in the stirrup. When he had a solid hold with his elbow, he gripped his wrist to keep his arm from slipping out and looked up at the horse. Clucking his tongue, he told the animal, "Okay, boy. Nice and easy. Take me home."

The big animal had gone only a few feet when a dizzy spell washed over Hoffman and he lost his grip. Lying on his back in utter despair, he listened to his horse whinnying. The mule, which was a few paces behind, nickered. The rancher was about to try again when he heard hoofbeats drawing near. Though his eyes were not focusing properly, he saw the form of a man slide from a horse and stand over him. The man, whose face was in shadow and silhouetted against the setting sun, said nothing.

Sighing with relief that someone had found him, Hoffman gasped, "Thank God you've come along! A . . . a grizzly got hold of me! I live . . . just a little ways west of here. If . . . you could help me to my place . . ."

Hoffman peered up at the man, who remained silent, and he struggled to bring him into focus. He started to speak again when he heard the click of a hammer being cocked. At the sight of the rider pointing a black muzzle at his chest, a cold ball rose in the pit of his stomach, freezing his insides. His eyes bulged and a trembling shook him as he tried to speak, but his fear prevented it. His "rescuer" was going to kill him. Shifting slightly, he finally saw the man's face clearly, and he felt the shock race all through his body.

For a frozen, eternal second the rancher waited for the blast—and then it came. His attacker laughed fiendishly, obviously thinking that he had killed Hoffman, and he mounted and rode away.

Hoffman's chest was on fire, and he was amazed to still be alive. The bullet had missed his heart, but when he coughed, blood erupted with a brassy taste inside his mouth. No doubt a lung had been punctured. He did not know how long he could last, but he was determined to make it to the house and tell Emmy who had shot him.

Struggling once again to hook his arm in the stirrup, the mortally wounded rancher commanded his horse to take him home. Hoffman fought to stay conscious, and after what seemed a lifetime the horse dragged him into the yard and stopped at the back porch. Bleeding profusely, Hoffman crawled up the steps of the porch, calling weakly, "Emmy! Emmy!" The effort caused him to cough again, and he spit up blood.

He lay still for a moment, waiting for Emmy's response, but there was none. His blood was pooling on the porch floor beneath him, and he knew that at the rate he was losing blood, he would be dead in minutes. Calling to his wife repeatedly, he crawled to the door. It took a great effort to reach up and turn the knob, but he was eventually able to twist it and the door came open.

Slithering into the kitchen, he called for Emmy again, but still there was no response. Laying his head on an arm, he rested, breathing heavily. At that moment he remembered the trouble at the Farnham ranch and assumed Emmy had taken the children and gone over there.

Not much time, he told himself. *I'm going to die, but I must tell Emmy who killed me. Somehow I must leave a message.* The dying man raised his head and looked around the kitchen. There had to be a way, he thought. His gaze fell on a folded newspaper that lay on the cupboard counter, part of it dangling over the edge. Inching toward the cupboard, he fought against the painful thoughts stabbing at his mind, thoughts of leaving his wife a widow and his children fatherless.

Focusing on reaching the newspaper, Hoffman clawed his way to a sitting position and leaned against the cupboard. He coughed and choked on the blood oozing into his mouth, then reached up with trembling fingers and tried to grasp the corner of the newspaper. Focusing was difficult, and he could not seem to put his hand where it needed to be to pinch the paper between his fingers. In desperation, he swung at the newspaper with an open hand, and it sailed off the counter onto the floor.

Gasping, Hoffman slid along the floor to the paper. He reached it and spread it open, all the while battling blacking out. *No! I mustn't die yet!* he shouted at himself.

Willing his mind clear, he dipped his forefinger to his bullet wound, and using his own blood, he wrote the letter *K*. He repeated the endeavor until he had finished the word *killer* and began following the word with a name.

His hand was soaked with blood and he was losing the last of his strength, but desperate to complete the task, he lowered his quivering hand and finished the name. Suddenly a terrible stab of pain lanced his chest. Jerking, he collapsed, and as he fell, his bloody hand smeared the name, leaving for a clue only that Vic Hoffman had known the person who had murdered him.

At the Farnham ranch Deputy Sheriff Buck Durand paced the parlor floor. A pallid Beth Farnham sat on the sofa, flanked by Emmy Hoffman and Hank Farnham. Noting that the light was fading outside, Buck stopped pacing and said, "Mrs. Farnham, it looks like Ron may not be coming home. It's almost dark, and I've got to report what happened to Sheriff Stenner, and—well, I'm sorry, but we'll have to hunt Ron down. I don't like leaving you and Hank here alone, though. Is there someone you can stay with in Lander?"

Beth was about to answer when Emmy suggested, "They can come back with me to my house, Buck. Vic will be there by now, and he'll welcome them. Even if Ron shows up there, he won't try anything with Vic around."

After agreeing to spend the night at the Hoffman home, and leaving Willie's body on his bed for the time being, Beth and Hank climbed in the Hoffman wagon with

Emmy and her children. With the deputy riding alongside, they headed for the neighboring ranch through the gathering darkness.

As they pulled onto the road, Buck said, "Mrs. Farnham, if you wish, I'll contact Sidney Jager for you when I get to town. He can come out and pick up Willie's body in the morning. I assume you will want him to prepare the body for burial and provide the coffin."

Solemnly, Beth replied, "Yes, Buck. Please tell Mr. Jager to take care of it. I'll talk to him as soon as possible."

They had gone just a short distance when they saw a riderless horse standing near the stand of cottonwood trees and a crumpled form lying at the side of the road. As the deputy spurred his horse, Hank blurted, "Ma, that's Ron's horse!"

By the time the wagon reached the spot, Buck was on the ground, kneeling beside Ron Farnham's body. Hank bounded from the vehicle and dropped beside him, while Beth burst into sobs, bewailing the loss of a second son.

"He was shot in the chest," Buck muttered. "You can tell he died instantly 'cause there's hardly any blood. The bullet went right through his heart."

Too stunned to even cry, Hank walked back to his mother. While he and Emmy worked at comforting her, Buck hoisted the dead man's body onto his own horse and draped it over the saddle. The Hoffman children observed the scene in wide-eyed silence.

Gaining control of her emotions, Beth stared at the deputy and in an anguished voice asked, "Who would have shot Ron? Who would have done this?"

"I wish I knew, ma'am," replied Buck. "Sheriff Stenner and I will ride out here at first light. We'll see if we can find anything that will help us catch your son's killer."

Sniffling, Beth said, "I want to take Ron's body home. Hank and I will stay there."

Emmy squeezed her friend's hand and protested,

"You and Hank shouldn't be in that house alone tonight—not with your sons' bodies."

"Please, Emmy," said the distraught mother, tears spilling from her eyes, "it will be the last time I will ever have my three boys together. Hank and I have nothing to fear now. This is the way I want it."

Bowing to Beth's wishes, Emmy turned the wagon around and, with the deputy's horse bearing Ron's corpse, drove back to the ranch. After the youth's body had been placed on his bed, Buck told Beth he would see Emmy and the children home, then ride hard for town. He would send the Reverend Mr. Wright to the Farnham place right away and advise Sid Jager to pick up the bodies in the morning.

Darkness was closing in when Emmy turned the wagon into her yard with the deputy riding alongside. The house was completely dark, and in the deepening dusk they could just make out Hoffman's horse and pack mule standing by the back porch.

"That's strange," Emmy said to Buck as she quickly hauled the wagon to a halt. "Vic never leaves his horse standing free like this. And why aren't there any lamps lit? Something's wrong."

"Mommy, where's Daddy?" Bobby asked from the wagon bed.

"I don't know, honey," she responded. "Maybe he's not feeling well. Perhaps he went right to bed."

Peering through the darkness, Buck tried to see if the deer was hanging from any of the trees that surrounded the yard. There was no sign of it. He dismounted, helped Emmy from the wagon, then lifted the children out.

Emmy took her four-year-old daughter into her arms, crossing quickly onto the porch, and Buck moved ahead to open the door but found it already ajar. Emmy's voice quavered as she said softly, so as not to alarm the children, "Buck, I don't like the looks of this. Vic wouldn't have left the door open in this cold. I just know something is wrong."

"Let's not jump to conclusions," Buck offered. "Is there a lamp close by?"

"There's one on the table," Emmy replied, putting down her daughter and moving through the door into the blackness of the kitchen.

"Mommy, I'm scared," spoke up Bobby.

"There's nothing to be afraid of," the young mother said lightly as she walked with easy familiarity to the table. "Mommy will have the light on in just a minute."

Buck waited just inside the door with the children as Emmy grasped the lamp. She removed the glass chimney, holding on to the base, and with her other hand fumbled for a small box of matches that was always kept within reach on the cupboard. Unknowingly, her right foot was but inches from her husband's body. Removing a match, she struck it on the edge of the cupboard.

The flame immediately illuminated the corpse on the floor. Emmy screamed sharply and dropped the match, and it hit the floor and went out. Buck bounded across the floor, having seen the body in the brief flash of light, while the children began screaming in terror.

Buck bumped into the table in an effort to avoid stepping on the body. Taking hold of Emmy, whose screams were unrelenting, he held her in his arm while he fumbled for the matches. Releasing her, he found the lamp, struck a match, and lit the wick.

The wails of the children intensified as the room came alive with light, and they ran across the room and wrapped their arms around their mother's legs and stared at the bloody body of their father. Collecting herself enough to minister to her children, Emmy cried, "Don't look! Don't look!"

Obediently, the children buried their faces in Emmy's skirt.

Shaking all over, she stood watching the deputy as he

bent over her husband's lifeless body. Her breath came in heavy gasps as each hand clutched a terrified child.

Feeling a wave of nausea slide through his stomach, Buck rolled the body onto its back. Blood was everywhere. The awful sight made the deputy go numb all over, and there was a cold, hollow feeling in his chest. The grisly object at his feet had been a healthy, happy human being when he had left him on the mountain a few short hours ago.

Emmy's bulging eyes were riveted on the bloody corpse. Stepping to her, Buck murmured, "Ma'am, let me take you and the children into the parlor." Without waiting for her consent, he held her arm firmly with one hand and grabbed the lamp with the other and ushered the stunned woman into the dark shadows of the parlor, her children still clutching her skirt. When Buck had seated Emmy on a couch, he lit the lamp on one side table and put the other lamp on the matching table. Pulling up a straight-backed chair, he sat down in front of her and gripped her trembling hands.

She was still too shocked to cry and only stared at the young lawman and mumbled, "What . . . what h-happened to my h-husband?"

"I need to take a closer look before I can be sure," replied Buck, who was feeling queasy himself. "Will you be all right if I leave you alone for a few minutes?"

"Yes. I . . . I'll be all right," Emmy assured him. "Please . . . check him closely and see what you can find out."

Picking up one of the lamps, Buck went back to the kitchen. After about ten minutes he returned to the parlor and sat down facing Emmy. "Vic was mauled by some kind of wild animal, Mrs. Hoffman. A bear, I would say. Probably a grizzly. His face and chest have many claw marks."

"Oh, how awful!" she gasped, biting her lip. "My poor darling must have suffered horribly!"

"Yes, ma'am"—he paused—"but there's more."

"What do you mean?"

"It wasn't the grizzly that killed your husband, Mrs. Hoffman. He was shot in the chest . . . just like Ron Farnham."

Emmy looked at him incredulously. "What are you saying?"

"I think that we have some kind of a deranged killer on the loose. Did you notice the newspaper on the floor next to . . . to Vic's body?"

"No," she said, shuddering.

"Well, he wrote a message on the newspaper with his own blood before he died. He knew the man that shot him."

Emmy's mouth dropped open. "You mean Vic wrote the name of his killer on the paper? Who did it, Buck?" she demanded. *"Who did it?"*

Shaking his head slowly, Buck replied dolefully, "The name is illegible. Vic wrote the word 'killer' and then the name, but the name got smeared. It can't be read."

Emmy began to weep. "Then my husband's murderer will go free."

His jaw tightening with anger, Buck promised, "We'll catch him anyway. Sheriff Stenner and I will soon be on the man's trail and we'll catch him. I guarantee it."

After taking the grieving widow and her two children into Lander to stay with friends, Deputy Buck Durand rode to the parsonage of the Methodist Church—Lander's only church—and informed the Reverend Cecil Wright of the three deaths. The Reverend Mr. Wright, a tall and gangly man with a pockmarked face and a protruding Adam's apple, was visibly shaken. Rubbing his sharp, beaklike nose, he told Buck he would first see Emmy Hoffman, and then he would ride to the Farnham ranch to console Beth and Hank.

Knowing that the sheriff should immediately be in-

formed of the murders, Buck hurried to the Stenner house
before going to the undertaking parlor. When he reined in
at the sheriff's home, which seemed to have light spilling
from every window, the young lawman saw that Dr. John
Bristol's horse was tied at the gate. Buck dismounted and
strode up the walk and stepped onto the porch. Taking a
deep breath, he knocked and waited.

Soon rapid footsteps sounded, and Sheriff Bob Stenner
pulled the door open. A tall, slender man in his early
forties, Stenner nodded grimly at his deputy and stepped
back, saying, "Come in, Buck. You find Ron Farnham?"

"Yes, sir."

"Put him in jail?"

"No, sir," Buck replied, moving inside.

Looking surprised as he closed the door, Stenner
queried, "Why not? Doc told me what happened. The
man's guilty of manslaughter, Buck. He's got to be arrested."

Removing his hat, Buck explained, "I couldn't arrest
him when I found him, Sheriff. Ron's dead."

"Dead?" echoed Stenner, his eyes wide.

"Murdered. Shot through the heart. I found him
lying on the road not far from the Hoffman place." He
paused. "And that's not all. Vic Hoffman was murdered,
too."

Stenner's face paled. *"What?"*

At that moment footsteps were heard coming from
the back of the house, and beautiful Jenny Bristol appeared, her large dark-brown eyes filling with love at the
sight of the young lawman.

Sheriff Stenner's attention was riveted on his deputy.
"How was Vic Hoffman killed?" he demanded.

Buck pulled his gaze away from Jenny—whose eyes
widened with horror at the sheriff's words—and answered,
"He was shot in the chest . . . just like Ron Farnham."

Jenny's hands went to her mouth. The young woman's head bowed and her long black hair fell over her face.

"Oh, how horrible!" she exclaimed. Looking up again, she asked, "What happened?"

Reaching for Jenny's shoulder, Buck drew her close and said, "Both Vic and Ron were murdered sometime late in the day—I'm sure by the same person."

John Bristol appeared in the hallway and assessed the three figures standing just inside the front door. "Would someone mind telling me what's going on?" he asked.

Bristol's face reflected his shock and grief when Buck told him the news. Going into the parlor, they all sat down, and the deputy gave them the details of the murders, including how the rancher had written in his own blood his killer's name on the newspaper. The anticipation visible in all three faces quickly dwindled when Buck added that the name had been smeared, completely obliterating the killer's identity.

The deputy concluded his story by explaining that Beth Farnham and her only remaining son had requested to stay in their house with the bodies, and Emmy Hoffman and her children were in town at the Jed Murphy home.

Doc Bristol put on his coat and hat, picked up his bag, and said, "Bob, Corrie's fever is still high, but she's sleeping right now. I'd better go see Emmy. She might need my help. Jenny can stay here until it's time for Errol to pick her up for the dance."

Flicking a glance at Buck, Jenny said, "Father, I don't have to go to the dance. If you think I should stay with Corrie, I'll explain it to Errol. He'll understand."

The sheriff spoke up. "There's not going to be any dance, Jenny. I've got to call it off. With two murders having been committed today in our valley, not only would it be disrespectful to the dead to have the dance, but it might also be dangerous. We've got a killer on the loose, and there's no telling if he's going to strike again. I'll station someone at the town hall to explain everything and send the people home."

Jenny offered to stay the night and nurse Corrie if the sheriff so desired, and Stenner accepted. "Good," Bristol commented. "That makes me more comfortable about leaving. I'll be back to check on my patient at sunup."

As soon as the doctor had left, Buck mentioned that he had to go inform Sid Jager of the bodies he was to pick up in the morning. "Well," Stenner put in, "since I need to station someone at the town hall, let's walk together and we can discuss this case."

"Yes, sir." Turning to Jenny, Buck told her he would see her when he came back to get his horse, and the two lawmen left, closing the door behind them.

Jenny Bristol had been sitting in Corrie Stenner's bedroom, caring for the sleeping patient, when she heard a rap at the front door. Putting down the wet cloth she had been holding to Corrie's fevered brow, Jenny moved through the house to answer the knock. She was sure it would be Errol Durand, and upon opening the door, she found she was correct.

Errol was clearly upset as he stepped inside. Taking off his Stetson, he ran nervous fingers through his sandy hair, and looking down at Jenny, he said, "I feel really bad about Willie Farnham dying and about Ron and Vic being murdered. And I believe the sheriff did the right thing by canceling the dance, but . . . well, I'm really disappointed that things turned out this way."

The young brunette replied softly, "It's all so terrible, Errol. I sure hope the sheriff can track down the killer quickly."

"Yeah, me, too," he agreed with a nod, gazing around the room.

"What are you looking for?" Jenny asked.

"I . . . uh . . . I saw Buck's horse out front. Is he here?"

"No. He was, but he left with Sheriff Stenner. He had to go tell Sid Jager about the bodies."

"Oh," the older Durand brother breathed, noticeably relieved. Turning his hat nervously in his hands, he said, "Jenny, I . . . I had planned to have a talk with you after the dance tonight, but since there won't be a dance, could we talk right now?"

Jenny glanced in the direction of Corrie's room, then looked back at Errol and replied, "I really can't. Corrie's still quite fevered, and I've got to bring her temperature down. Could we make it some other time?"

"Well, I guess so. It's something very important, but I understand. Real soon, though, okay?"

"Sure. Maybe in a day or two."

Obviously keenly disappointed, Errol left.

Jenny had been alone about twenty minutes when the two lawmen returned, and the young woman informed the sheriff that Corrie was still sleeping. Stenner looked at the young couple gazing longingly at each other, and he excused himself, saying, "I think I'll go back and sit with Corrie for a while."

When they were alone in the parlor, Buck took Jenny in his arms and kissed her. They then sat on the couch and she told him, "Errol was here while you were gone."

"I figured he would show up, since the dance was canceled. Did you tell him about us?"

"No. When I do, I want to do it right, so I'll need some time to talk to him, and I just couldn't leave Corrie alone that long."

Nodding, Buck remarked, "I appreciate your wanting to make it as easy as possible on Errol." His brow furrowed as he added, "I wish my brother didn't have to get hurt. It's too bad you don't have a sister he could fall in love with."

A strange expression came over Jenny's face, and she looked away from Buck.

"What's the matter, darling?" he asked.

The young woman took a deep breath and fought

back the tears that had rushed into her eyes. She tried to speak, but could not for the lump in her throat.

Seeing that she was distressed, Buck took both of her hands in his own and lifted her chin to look into her eyes. "Please, Jenny. What is it?"

Freeing one hand, she wiped away a tear trickling down her cheek. "Buck, I . . . I'm not supposed to be telling anyone this. Father wanted it kept secret. But . . . well, you're the man I love, and I don't think I should keep anything from you. I need you to promise, though, that you'll never tell this to anyone else."

"If that's what you want, you have my promise. What is it?"

Jenny's lower lip quivered as she wiped away another tear and said, "I *do* have a sister—but she'll never be anyone's wife. Her name is Lucinda, and she's two years older than I am. She—"

Jenny's voice broke. It took a few moments for her to collect herself; then, continuing, she brushed a lock of black hair from her eyes and said, "She lives in San Francisco, Buck. She . . . she's in an asylum for the insane."

"Oh, Jenny, I'm sorry," the young lawman said tenderly. "You don't have to tell me more, if you don't want to."

"No, I want you to know." She sighed deeply before going on. "We lived in San Francisco, where my father had a good practice. Lucinda was normal; then suddenly one night eight years ago, when I was thirteen and she was fifteen, she did a horrible thing. I was at a girlfriend's house, staying the night, and Father was out tending a very sick patient. Mother and Lucinda were home alone, and since Father and I were not there, we don't know exactly what happened, but something unbalanced Lucinda's mind. She went into a fit of rage and"—Jenny drew a deep, shuddering breath—"she stabbed Mother to death."

"How horrible!" Buck exclaimed, shaking his head.

"It was a nightmare. Father was very late getting

home that night, and when he arrived and found Mother dead, Lucinda was sitting beside the body in a catatonic state, staring blankly into space. She had lost all sense of reality. My poor father had the awful task of having to commit her to the asylum, and I haven't seen her since they took her away. I . . . I lived in fear for a long time that if my sister had become mad, it might happen to me. By the time I turned twenty and I was still normal, the fear went away."

"That's good," commented the deputy, patting her hand. "I'm sure it must have been something that was exclusively within Lucinda's own personality."

"Anyway, when the story came out in the newspapers, Father found it hard to face the community. We moved across the bay to Oakland, and he started a new practice there, but it wasn't long until people there began to talk. It didn't seem to hurt Father's practice, but it was becoming very difficult for me. You know how schoolchildren are. They began to taunt me unmercifully about having a crazy sister. So we moved farther north, to Sacramento, and everything was fine until about three years ago when Father again started hearing the gossip about Lucinda. It was then that he decided it would be best for us to leave the state."

"So what brought you to Lander?"

"I'm sure you remember Dr. Holcomb, who had a practice here. Well, he died suddenly, and he and Father had a mutual friend who knew of our troubles. The friend told Father about Dr. Holcomb's death, and we came here to start a new life."

"I'm sure glad you did," Buck stated with a smile. His face grew sober again, and he said, "I remember that when we first met, you told me your mother was dead, but I just assumed that she died of natural causes."

Tears glistened in Jenny's big brown eyes as she looked at the man she loved. "Buck . . ."

"Yes?"

"It . . . it doesn't make any difference how you feel about me, does it? Knowing I have a sister who is insane, I mean."

Folding her into his arms, Buck warmed her with a gentle kiss. "Absolutely not," he assured her. "I love you for who and what *you* are. Nothing else matters."

Chapter Six

The next morning a cold wind whipped across the valley beneath a leaden sky that presaged snow. Just after daybreak Dr. John Bristol walked toward the Stenner house, carrying his black leather bag.

A small dog charged off a porch, barking at the physician ferociously, but Bristol paid no attention to it. Hunching down into his coat collar, he bent his head against the wind and pressed on. As he stepped inside the gate at the Stenner yard, he glanced up at the gray sky, expecting it to start spitting snow any minute.

Jenny answered the door at his knock and smiled as he entered. Closing the door, she hugged him and asked, "How's my favorite father this morning?"

Bristol kissed her cheek and responded, "How could I be anything but fine, having a daughter like you?" Removing his coat and hat, he asked, "How's Corrie?"

Smiling, the young woman replied, "I'm happy to tell you that her fever broke during the night. She's doing much better now."

"Wonderful!" said the doctor. "That's a relief. I'll go in and take a look at her. Is Bob awake?"

"Yes. He's shaving in the spare bedroom where he

spent the night, while I slept on a cot in the room with Corrie. You go check on your patient and I'll start breakfast."

Bristol headed for Corrie's bedroom, bearing his black bag, and Jenny went to the kitchen. Moments later she was interrupted by a knock at the front door. Wiping biscuit batter from her hands on her apron, she hurried to the door. Pulling it open, she smiled at the handsome sandy-haired deputy standing before her. "Good morning, Buck. I love you."

Stepping inside, the young lawman responded, "I love you, too, darling."

After glancing around to see that they were alone, he swept her into his arms and kissed her soundly. Then, following her farther into the kitchen, he said, "I thought I'd come over and see if the sheriff wants me to take him out to the spot where Ron Farnham was shot."

At that moment the lanky sheriff appeared and said, "Good morning, Buck. I heard what you said, but I'll do my investigating alone. By now everyone in town knows there's a killer running loose around here, and folks are bound to be edgy. It'd be best if they've got one lawman close by. You can just draw me a map and show me where you found Ron. I also want to examine the Hoffman kitchen, where Vic died."

"Whatever you say, Sheriff," Buck responded. "You'll find everything in Vic's kitchen just as I found it, except that I turned his body over to look at it, and before we left I covered it with a blanket."

"Fine. By the way, I want to get there before Sid Jager takes the body. Did he mention to you when he'd be leaving?"

"He told me last night that it would be late morning before he could get out there."

"That'll work out fine then. As soon as Jenny feeds me some breakfast, I'll be on my way. Did you eat yet?"

Looking a bit sheepish, the deputy replied, "Uh, as a matter of fact, no. I figured Jenny would be cooking breakfast here this morning, so I hoped I'd get an invite to partake while I was here."

Dr. John Bristol entered the kitchen just then and admitted, "Me, too. Since my daughter wasn't home to cook my breakfast, I figured the least you could do, Bob, was let me plant my feet under your table. And you'll be pleased to know that Corrie is well on the mend, which means *she'll* be back to cooking your breakfast for you in a day or two."

Stenner was elated. "That's wonderful news!" he exclaimed. "And you two are more than welcome to share my breakfast with me." Grinning at Jenny, the lawman added playfully, "Of course, I'll miss having this beautiful young woman taking care of me, but . . ."

While they ate, the deputy drew a map of the spot where Ron had been shot and gave it to the sheriff. As soon as breakfast was over, both Bristol and Stenner departed, leaving Jenny and Buck alone. The deputy helped her clean up the table, then said, "Well, I guess I'd better be getting to the office." As he spoke, he moved close and took hold of her hand. "But before I go, there's something I have to take care of."

"What's that?" she asked, a quizzical look on her face.

"I haven't made a formal proposal yet, and it must not be delayed any longer. Therefore"—he loudly cleared his throat—"Miss Jenny Bristol, will you marry me?"

The young brunette accepted the proposal with a warm kiss. When they parted, Buck declared, "You've just made me the happiest man in the whole world! But are you sure you want to marry a lawman? It's not like being married to a shopkeeper or even a doctor, you know."

"I know," Jenny responded, nodding. "My maternal grandfather was a lawman, so I know about the strain and the hardships of it. Grandfather was marshal for many years in a mighty tough town, but he lived to retire."

Buck smiled. "Well, then, I guess you know what you're getting into."

"Yep. It will be exciting, I'm sure, but I would marry you no matter what you did for a living."

After kissing her again, Buck put on his coat and headed for the door. As she followed him he said, "Honey, if you'd rather it was me who told Errol about us, I'll be glad to do it."

She shook her head firmly. "I appreciate the offer, but it's my responsibility. I'm sure I'll have the opportunity within a day or two."

Before opening the door he suggested, "We haven't eaten at the hotel restaurant in a long time. How about letting me take you there tonight for dinner?"

"It's a date," she agreed, smiling. "With Corrie getting better, I'll probably go home sometime this afternoon. Come for me there. Say around six."

"Will you have to fix your dad's supper?"

"No. Mrs. Welch, our housekeeper, can do it. Father doesn't like her cooking nearly as well as mine, but one meal won't hurt him."

Buck kissed Jenny one more time, then headed for the sheriff's office. On the way he met the Reverend Cecil Wright, who told him he had been at the Farnham place until quite late last night, for Beth was having a hard time. The additional news of Vic Hoffman's murder had added to her grief. The preacher was just on his way to see Emmy Hoffman and assist her in making funeral arrangements.

Nodding solemnly, the young lawman continued on. By the time he reached the office, snow was beginning to fall.

The light snow gave the Hoffman property a pristine look as Sheriff Bob Stenner veered off the road and into the yard. He dreaded having to go in and look at the body of his longtime friend, and sadness filled his heart, as he knew he would never again enjoy Vic Hoffman's company. Easing from the saddle, he took a deep breath and let it out slowly, then stepped onto the porch.

As he did so he saw the trail of blood and the spot where the blood had pooled near the door. His stomach went sour. Taking a few seconds to brace himself, he opened the door and stepped inside.

His throat constricted as he beheld the lifeless form covered with a blanket. Walking slowly, he lifted the blanket from the corpse and laid it on a chair, and bitter bile filled his mouth when he stared at the bloody thing that yesterday had been his friend. He turned quickly away and stepped to a window to look outside, waiting for his stomach to settle. Grief lanced his heart, and he had to fight to keep from bursting into sobs.

After several minutes Stenner turned back to the body. Kneeling down, he scrutinized the newspaper, reading the word *killer* and swearing when he was unable to read the killer's name. He gritted his teeth and looked into Hoffman's stone-cold face, saying, "You tried to tell us who did it, old pal. You knew him. Well, don't you worry. I'm going to get him. If it's the last thing I do, I'm going to get him."

The sheriff studied the kitchen carefully but could find nothing that told him any more about the rancher's death. Picking up the blanket, he looked down at the corpse and said, "You must have given that grizzly a good fight, my friend. The fact that you got away from him tells me that. But your fight was all for nothing because of some murderous scum." Fighting back his tears, Stenner whispered, "Rest in peace, Vic."

Hurriedly covering the body with the blanket, the sheriff left the house and returned to his horse. He bent his head against the driving wind and rode out of the yard, heading toward the Farnham place. As he drew close to the farm he pulled out the map Buck Durand had drawn for him and studied it, and by the time he reached the spot where Ron Farnham had been cut down, the snow on the ground was deeper. Dismounting, he walked around the area, staring periodically through the falling snow into the gray haze of the forest, but-there was nothing anywhere to give a clue as to the identity of the man who had killed the hotheaded son of Beth Farnham.

The wind-driven snow was getting heavier as Stenner reached the Farnham ranch. Entering the house at Hank's invitation, he found the widow sitting in the parlor, deeply grieved and staring blankly through the window.

"Ma," Hank murmured, touching her shoulder, "Sheriff Stenner's here."

Beth turned her head slowly toward the lawman's compassionate gaze, but she seemed to be looking through him rather than seeing him. Her face was pale and haggard, and Stenner thought that she looked twenty years older than when he had seen her last.

"She isn't sayin' much, Sheriff," said Hank. "It got worse when the preacher told her about Vic Hoffman bein' murdered."

Bending down to Beth's level, Stenner looked into her dull eyes and said, "Mrs. Farnham, I know words are poor vehicles of comfort at a time like this . . . but they're all we have. I want to tell you how sorry I am about Willie and Ron. I know you're hurting something awful right now. Please know that you have my deepest sympathy."

Beth's eyes suddenly focused on him. "Thank you, Sheriff," she said, so softly he had to strain to hear her. "I appreciate your kindness. Is your wife feeling any better? Emmy told me about her being sick."

"Yes, ma'am, she is," replied Stenner. "Her fever broke, so she'll be all right now."

"That's good. Have you seen Emmy this morning?"

"No, ma'am, but I'm sure the Murphys are being a great help to her."

Beth merely nodded.

Hank asked if the sheriff had learned anything, but Stenner reported that so far he had found nothing. He was just as bewildered as they were as to who in the valley would want to kill either man. Try as he might, he could not come up with one good solid suspect.

Donning his hat, the lawman told the Farnhams, "I have to go now, but I want you to know that I will do everything in my power to bring the killer to justice."

He bid them good-bye and hurried outside. Mounting up, Bob Stenner gave a brief wave at the two sad faces gazing at him from the window, his own sorrow evident.

Watching from behind a stand of pines, a shadowy figure laughed fiendishly. Just before the lawman turned his horse around and prodded the animal into a trot, the killer lashed his mount and sped up the road toward town.

Eager to get back to town and out of the storm, Stenner decided to take a shortcut through the woods that would cut off nearly three miles. As he slowly threaded his way through the trees, the sheriff recalled the many happy times he had spent with Vic Hoffman in those woods. With each memory he felt Hoffman's loss even deeper—which made him all the more determined to find and arrest the man who had killed his friend in what he assumed was cold blood. It would be a pleasure to see him take the drop at the end of a rope.

Stenner's mind dwelled on why anyone would want to kill either man. Ron had been a troublemaker ever since he was a small boy and had provoked many a fistfight, but nothing was bad enough to kill him over, and he had even proven himself valuable while riding in posses. And there had been nothing about Vic Hoffman to make anyone want to kill him, for he was the nicest of nice guys.

Suddenly Stenner saw movement just ahead of him. Drawing back on the reins, he blinked and peered through the falling, swirling snow. He was about to believe his eyes were playing tricks on him when a dark form stepped out from behind a tree with a revolver aimed at Stenner's chest. The man was no more than twenty feet away, but his face was obscured in the shadow of his hat brim. Stenner's heart leapt in his breast, for he knew without question that he was facing the killer. Going for his gun, his hand flashed toward his hip, but the killer's gun roared, blossoming orange in the deep shade of the forest.

Stenner jerked as the slug tore into his chest. The murderer stepped closer, snapping back the hammer and keeping the smoking muzzle aimed at the lawman. Recognition showed in the sheriff's glazing eyes just before he died and peeled from the saddle onto the snow-covered ground.

The killer stood over him, laughed with glee, eased the hammer down on his gun, and walked over to his horse.

The wind had dwindled to a slight breeze by midmorning, though snow was still falling moderately. Heading for Lander, Errol Durand had decided he could wait no longer. He was going to ask Jenny Bristol to marry him.

He was within a quarter mile of town when he saw a rider coming toward him from the west. It took only seconds to recognize the chestnut gelding with four white stockings as that of his friend Ford Loker. "Howdy, Ford," Errol said as they drew abreast.

"Howdy," Loker repeated. Opening his hands so that the snow fell onto his palms, he quipped, "Some day off, huh?"

Errol chuckled. "Judging from the direction you've come from, I don't think you've let a little snow keep you from doing what you usually do on your day off. Does this little filly live on one of the ranches out there, or is she a resident of a town west of here?"

"She lives on a ranch, old friend," Loker replied, grinning.

"Well, when will I get to meet her?"

"Not until you're married, pal. You're too good-looking for me to trust you around her unless you're already attached."

Errol laughed and said, "Well, if that's what's worrying you, your worries are about over. I'm on my way right now to pop the question to Jenny."

"Think you'll marry her pretty fast after she accepts?"

"Yep. We'll probably hitch up before Thanksgiving."

"Good luck. If it doesn't take you too long to get your answer, we can ride home together. I'll be at the Lone Pine Saloon."

The two men entered town and parted, with Errol making a beeline for the Bristol house, eager to propose to Jenny. His heart beat furiously as he stood on the porch and waited for Jenny to answer his knock. When the door opened, he found himself looking at the chubby face of Harriet Welch, Dr. Bristol's housekeeper.

"Morning, Mrs. Welch," he said, touching his hat brim. "Is Jenny in?"

"No, she isn't, Errol," replied the housekeeper pleasantly. "She's still over at the sheriff's house, where she stayed all night with Corrie."

Errol thanked the woman and quickly rode through the snow-covered streets to the Stenner house. Answering his knock, Jenny came to the door with a towel on each shoulder and a wet washrag in her hand. Errol frowned and said, "Looks like I'm showing up at a bad time again, Jenny."

"I'm afraid you're right. I'm in the midst of giving Corrie a sponge bath," Jenny explained. "Can you come by my house tomorrow night?"

Errol's countenance fell. "I really have something important to talk to you about. How about tonight?"

"I can't tonight. I have a dinner engagement with Buck."

The tall, muscular man sighed. "Well, then, can we have dinner tomorrow night?"

Jenny nodded. "Yes," she agreed. "Tomorrow night would be fine."

"I'll come by your house at six, okay?"

"Six it is," the brunette confirmed and closed the door.

His jaw set angrily, Errol Durand dashed down the

walk to his horse and leapt into his saddle. He trotted to Lander's main street, rounded the corner, and headed for the sheriff's office. Dismounting at the hitch rail, he hurriedly wrapped the reins around the rail and crossed the boardwalk, only to find the sheriff's office locked. He cursed under his breath and turned and headed back for his horse. Just as he reached the edge of the boardwalk, he spotted his brother coming in his direction from across the street.

"Good morning, big brother," Buck said as he drew near, brushing the snow from his jacket.

Errol waited till his sibling was on the boardwalk, then snapped, "Look, Buck, you've always had a good brain in your head. You ought to be smart enough to read the handwriting on the wall!"

Buck was puzzled by his brother's aggressive attitude, but he smiled and asked lightly, "What handwriting on what wall?"

Passersby began to stare as Errol's voice grew in volume and pitch. "The handwriting that says Jenny's in love with *me*, that's what, so there's no sense in stringing this out any longer. Why don't you break your date for tonight and let me take her out so I can talk to her?"

Feeling tempted to take it upon himself to tell his brother that *he* was the loser, the deputy nonetheless held his tongue since Jenny had insisted on telling Errol herself.

"So go to her right now and tell her your date for tonight is off!" Errol demanded.

The order was more than the deputy could take. Though Errol was older and bigger, Buck had never let him push him around, and he was not about to start now. His temper rising, the young lawman challenged, "Who do you think you are, telling me to break my date?"

"I'm the man Jenny's going to marry—that's who!"

Thinking carefully before retorting, and using words that would be close to the truth but not reveal it, young Durand countered, "Well, she hasn't told me anything about being engaged to you! Just when did this engagement take place? I was with her just this morning and she didn't say anything about it!"

Errol was clearly nonplussed, and he looked around at the onlookers who had stopped to stare at the brothers, despite the falling snow. One of those watching was Ford Loker, who had heard the argument from inside the saloon.

His face stiffening with the rage that had flooded to the surface, Errol's fist abruptly lashed out and cracked his sibling on the jaw, knocking Buck backward into the street. The young rancher strode off the boardwalk and stood over his rival, fists balled and ready for action. Narrowing his eyes, he warned menacingly, "Unless you're ready to get knocked down again, little brother, you'd better stay down!"

Defiance was written on Buck's face, which darkened with anger. He was usually hard to rile, but when his temper was up, he could be dangerous. The unexpected punch had cut his lip on the inside of his mouth, and he tasted the tang of blood—as well as bitterness. Glaring at his older brother, he sprang to his feet, spit blood in the street, and blared, "You started it, but I'm going to finish it!"

As Buck closed in, his adversary unleashed a haymaker, but the smaller man ducked it and smashed Errol savagely on the nose. A woman in the gathering crowd gasped as Errol backpedaled from the impact of the blow, stumbled on the edge of the boardwalk, and fell flat on his back. Shaking his head, he swore at Buck and got up breathing heavily, blood bubbling from both nostrils.

Enraged, he charged, but Buck met him halfway, swinging a powerful right. The punch connected, but the snow under the deputy's feet caused him to lose his balance, and while Errol went down from the punch, Buck went down from the slip. The elder Durand got up first and kicked his brother in the rib cage as he was rising, knocking the breath from the young lawman and felling him, causing him to clutch his side. A moan rose from the crowd when Errol again kicked his brother in the same place.

Pain shot through Buck's whole body, but he was able to reach out and grab Errol's foot, and giving it a wild twist, he threw him to the ground. While Errol lay on his back, the deputy rose, gasping for breath, and demanded, "Get up, big brother! I said I'm going to finish this fight!"

The older Durand complied, and the two men continued fighting, their brutality astonishing the onlookers. Finally, Buck seemed to be gaining the upper hand, wearing down Errol little by little.

Watching the bleeding and battered brothers, Ford Loker realized that while he had hoped to see Errol beat his younger sibling to a pulp, the fight was going the other way, and his friend would be hammered down if the fight was not stopped.

Loker pushed his way through the crowd to Virgil Orcutt. The fifty-five-year-old chairman of the town council was standing beside Mike Hanson, a younger councilman, and Loker slipped behind Orcutt and remarked, "I don't know where Sheriff Stenner is, but don't you think this thing oughtta be stopped before Errol gets hurt?"

Orcutt looked over his shoulder at Loker, then at Hanson, who nodded his agreement. "I think you're right, Ford," the council chairman concurred. Stepping into the street, he walked toward the combatants just as Errol went down hard. The older Durand was spitting blood and attempting to get up when Orcutt jumped in front of the deputy and said, "That's enough, Buck. You proved your point. You finished the fight."

One of Errol's eyes was swelling shut as he got to his knees. Nodding to Orcutt, the deputy stood over his brother and gasped, "I'm still . . . keeping my date . . . with Jenny tonight . . . big brother. Any . . . objections?"

Errol spit more blood but did not reply. He merely scowled at his brother as Loker helped him to his feet and escorted him to his horse.

Buck reached the sheriff's office with the two councilmen flanking him. Looking at each of them in turn, he explained, "Errol hit me first. I couldn't let him get away with it."

"We understand, Buck," Orcutt assured him. "You had to fight back. But it looked as though Errol would be seriously hurt if the fight continued, since you seemed pretty mad, so I stepped in."

The young lawman nodded wordlessly and stepped into the office, closing the door behind him. Looking at the closed door, Orcutt sighed and said to Hanson, "That rivalry over Jenny Bristol has gone on between those boys for quite a while. I guess it was bound to come to blows."

"Yeah," agreed Hanson. "But I don't know that it's just rivalry over Jenny that put all that fire in Buck's eyes—and his punches. I think he must have a lot of resentment stored up over losing such a large percentage of the inheritance."

"You may be right," responded Orcutt. He gloomily added, "The trouble between the Durand brothers may not be over yet."

Chapter Seven

Buck Durand was washing the blood from his face at the washbowl in the sheriff's office when the door opened. Turning, he saw Sidney Jager standing in the doorway and brushing snow from his shoulders. The short, stout undertaker then entered the room and walked to the stove, holding his hands over it for warmth.

Grabbing a towel and drying his face, Durand faced Jager and said, "Howdy, Sid."

"Howdy." Gesturing with his chin, the middle-aged Jager added, "Your face is gonna be one bruised mess, come tomorrow. I just heard about the fight. Does the victor get the girl, or is it still not settled?"

The deputy looked at the blood on the towel, dabbed at his face some more, and replied with assurance, "I doubt if Jenny's decision will be based on who can whip whom."

"So it's still not settled," Jager mumbled dryly. "Well, truthfully, I figured you boys would have been pounding each other over that beautiful gal a long time ago."

Not wanting to discuss the matter any further, the young lawman asked, "You going after the bodies now?"

"Yes. I just came by to let the sheriff know that the

funerals for the Farnham boys and Vic Hoffman will be held at one o'clock tomorrow afternoon. I didn't see Bob's horse outside, so I guess he's not here. But when he gets back, will you tell him for me?"

"Sure will."

"Preacher Wright's the one that set the time. I just talked to him. He's already informed Beth and Emmy." Jager paused, then rubbed the back of his neck and said, "This whole thing's really terrible, isn't it?"

"Yeah," the deputy said bitterly. "Our peaceful valley isn't so peaceful anymore. Whoever this bloody monster is, he's got to be stopped. I can't for the life of me figure out why anyone would want to kill Ron and Vic."

Nodding, Jager allowed, "I find it real frightening that Vic recognized his killer. For all we know, so did Ron, if he had time to see him before he died."

Buck nodded. "It puts the shivers down my spine, Sid, to think that a cold-blooded murderer is walking among us . . . and we don't know he's the killer."

"It's disconcerting, all right," agreed the undertaker. "My heart really goes out to the families of the victims— especially those two women. Beth's already done a lot of suffering in her time, and it's a dirty shame that poor little Emmy should have to be a widow at such a young age."

Sighing, Jager took his leave of the deputy and drove away in the funeral wagon, heading south out of town.

Late that afternoon the snowstorm ended and the sky cleared, bringing with it colder air. A blast of it followed blacksmith Ken Chitwood through the door as he entered the sheriff's office, where Deputy Buck Durand was sweeping the floor, always his last chore before closing up for the day. Lifting his head and meeting Chitwood's gaze, the young lawman said, "Howdy, Ken. Looks like it's going to be a cold one tonight."

"That's for sure," agreed the thick-bodied smithy. At forty, Chitwood was as bald as an egg and as strong as a bull. "I was wonderin' if the sheriff found anything out there that would help identify the skunk who killed Ron and Vic. I was hopin' I'd have somethin' positive to report to my fellow council members."

Picking up the dustpan and sweeping dirt into it, Durand responded, "He hasn't been back since he rode out this morning. I figure he must have gone straight home to spend some time with Corrie instead of coming by the office. I'm heading over there right now, if you want to come along."

"I won't have time," responded Chitwood. "My missus gets her nose out of joint if I'm late for supper. Tell Bob I'll see him in the mornin'."

"Will do," the deputy said as the blacksmith headed for the door.

Putting on his coat and hat, Durand stepped out of the office and locked the door. The sun was getting nearer the western horizon, and as the light faded, the temperature dropped.

Plodding through three inches of new snow, the deputy made his way to the Stenner house and was surprised when Jenny answered the door. Stepping inside, he commented, "I thought you'd be home getting ready for our date."

"As a matter of fact, I was about to leave."

"Is the sheriff home, honey?"

The young brunette had been carefully studying Buck's bruised face, but the question clearly caught her off guard. "No, we haven't seen him all day," she answered, a perplexed expression on her face. "Corrie and I assumed he was busy at the office. But what happened to *you*?"

"I got into a little fight," he answered dismissively. "You don't suppose the sheriff has run into some kind of trouble? He hasn't been back to the office since he left this morning."

"Maybe he went to see Beth and Hank. What kind of fight?" she persisted.

"I wouldn't think he'd stay out there that long," he responded, ignoring her question.

"Sheriff Stenner is a very capable man. And it looks like it was more than a little fight to me. Who were you fighting?"

Buck knew his evasion was not going to work. He sighed and said, "My brother."

"What were you fighting about?"

"He demanded that I break our dinner date tonight so he could ask you to marry him. He said it's obvious that you're in love with him and that I might as well face it. When he got insistent, I saw red."

"Did you tell him about my decision?"

"No. I wanted to, but as mad as I was, I didn't. When I refused his demand, he hit me, and we went at it."

Jenny's face was filled with concern. "Oh, Buck, I'm sorry. You've been hurt because of me." She tenderly cupped his face in her hands and lightly kissed him on the lips. "Please forgive me. This is all my fault. I've known for months that it was you I'm in love with, and I should have told Errol the truth a long time ago. He's taking me to dinner tomorrow night, and I'll definitely tell him then."

"As far as I'm concerned, you don't need forgiving, sweetheart," the sandy-haired lawman said softly. "But I will be glad when Errol knows the truth." He kissed her lovingly, then looked toward the rear of the house, asking, "How's Corrie doing?"

"Fine. Her temperature is almost down to normal."

"That's great. Can I see her?"

"Sure. I know she'll be glad to see you."

When they entered the bedroom, two lamps were burning. Corrie Stenner was a tall, slender woman with dark-brown hair who normally was bursting with good health. But Durand thought that except for the dark circles under her eyes, her face was as white as the pillowcase under her head. She thought a great deal of the deputy and smiled warmly at him when he stepped to the bed. Extending her hand, she said quietly, "Hello, Buck."

"I'm sure glad to hear you're doing better," he declared, smiling back.

Her eyes were weary as she asked, "Did Bob come in with you?"

"No," replied the deputy, releasing her hand. "He's been out investigating those killings all day. He ought to be showing up soon."

They chatted for a few more minutes, and then Corrie said that she needed to rest. When Buck and Jenny returned to the parlor, he looked into her eyes and half-whispered, "Honey, I didn't want to let on to Corrie, but I'm really worried. The sheriff should have been back hours ago." He would not tell Jenny that scratching at the back of his mind was that two men were murdered the day before, and he feared the same thing had happened to Stenner. Calmly, he asked, "Would you forgive me if I break our dinner date tonight? I've got to go out to the Farnham place and see if Bob's still there."

Jenny kissed Durand, assuring him, "Of course I don't mind. I completely agree with you. I'll stay here until you get back."

The young lawman hurried out and mounted up. Reaching the Farnham house in the gathering darkness, his heart sank when he saw no sign of the sheriff's horse. Dismounting, he started walking toward the porch when the curtains parted at the illuminated window beside the door and a face appeared. Young Hank Farnham was looking out at him through the frosted glass, pressing his nose to the glass and squinting.

"It's Buck Durand, Hank!" called the deputy, stepping onto the porch.

Hank left the window and the door swung open. "Hi, Buck. Come in."

The youth closed the door behind the deputy, asking, "What're you doin' out here this time of day?"

Before Durand could answer, Beth Farnham entered the room, looking worn and exhausted. "Hello, Buck," she said, making an effort to smile. "To what do we owe this pleasure?"

"I'm looking for Sheriff Stenner, ma'am," he replied, having a hard time keeping the worry that clawed at his insides out of his voice. "Was he here earlier?"

"Yes. He arrived here—what time was it, Hank? —about nine-thirty this morning. He left around ten."

"That's right," confirmed Hank.

Beth studied the young lawman's blue eyes for a moment. "He hasn't come back to town?" she finally asked.

"No, ma'am. I was hoping he was still here."

"You don't suppose he returned to the Hoffman place? He told us that he'd been there before coming here, but maybe he had reason to go back."

"I can't imagine why he would need to stay there nearly all day," Durand mused, "but I'll sure drop over there and check."

The young deputy was becoming increasingly concerned as he rode away from the house and headed for the Hoffman ranch. The air was bitingly cold, and he could see his breath by the light of the full moon rising in the eastern sky. Putting his horse to a gallop, he soon arrived at the Hoffman place, and his concern mounted when he saw that no horse was tied at the porch and the house was completely dark.

Fearing the worst, he decided the best course of action was to get back to town immediately and recruit others to help him search for the sheriff, and he was grateful that the moonlight enabled him to take the shortcut through the woods. Reaching the edge of the forest, he veered off the road and picked his way between the dense trees. The shadows of the snow-covered pines and the nearly naked aspens were eerie, spectral patterns on the white mantle covering the forest. Thinking of the killer's running loose in the valley sent a prickly feeling slithering down the young lawman's spine, and he let his right hand drop close to the revolver on his hip.

Other than the slight breeze whispering through the treetops, the only sound in the forest was the crunching of his horse's hooves through the three-inch layer of snow. Then a horse whinnied suddenly somewhere off to his left, startling Buck, and he drew rein and listened. The whinny was repeated, and his own horse answered, lifting its ears and bobbing its head.

The young deputy's heart quickened pace. Whipping out his gun, he cocked the hammer. His horse nickered softly, lifting its head and stomping a hoof. "Easy, boy," Buck said softly, looking all around. The deep shadows that surrounded him seemed to have a thousand eyes, and if the killer was after him, he could be anywhere. Was the murderous fiend now stalking him as he had stalked Ron Farnham and Vic Hoffman? Maybe the man's horse had given him away.

Holding his gun ready, Buck directed his mount slowly forward in the direction of the other horse. He had gone about twenty yards when he saw movement farther ahead through the trees. Reining his horse, he held the animal still and peered through the heavy shadows. When the movement caught his eye again, he was able to determine that it was a horse's tail, swishing. Inching forward, he was soon able to see the entire horse, and when it turned slightly, showing the blaze on its nose, the deputy felt a sudden chill run through him. He was sure the horse was Sheriff Bob Stenner's, and the saddle was empty and snow covered.

Keeping the gun ready, Buck spurred his mount, and his breath caught painfully in his lungs when he spotted a shapeless, snow-blanketed heap on the ground beside the horse. Shuddering, he dismounted immediately and dashed to it, whispering hoarsely, "Oh, no!"

Easing the hammer into place, he slid his revolver into its holster and knelt beside the lifeless figure. The sheriff's hat had come off when he fell and lay a few feet away, covered with white. Buck picked it up with trembling hands, then brushed the snow from Stenner's face. Seeing the sheriff's wide-open, horror-filled eyes, Buck gasped, and he felt as though a hand were clutching his throat, squeezing down and cutting off his breath. His limbs suddenly seemed numb, and he felt as though he were unable to move. Tilting his head back, he opened his mouth, sucking hard to get air into his lungs. The arctic sting stimulated him, and the paralysis that had gripped him began to subside.

Buck Durand could scarcely believe the horrible situation was real. *Who would do a thing like this?* he asked himself. *What one man would want Ron Farnham, Vic Hoffman, and Sheriff Bob Stenner dead? Or is it more than one man? No. Hoffman wrote the singular "killer."*

Sighing with despair, he looked at the face of his friend and mentor. Buck would have to take Stenner's body into town, and he would have to tell Corrie that she was the latest widow. The deputy picked up the corpse and laid it facedown over the snowy saddle. He felt sick to his stomach. As he trudged to his own horse, a dreadful heaviness seemed to have turned his legs to lead. Settling in the saddle, he pictured Stenner's chest wound, remembering that there was hardly any blood. Mercifully, the sheriff had died instantly and had not suffered as Vic Hoffman did. Perhaps Corrie would find some slight comfort in that.

Grieved and angered, Buck led Stenner's horse into town. Keeping to the side streets, he rode up into the alley behind Sid Jager's undertaking parlor, and moments later he and Jager carried the body through the back door and laid it on the worktable.

Looking stunned, Jager eyed the deputy and asked, "What are you going to do?"

Buck scrubbed a shaky hand over his face and replied, "After I break the news to Corrie, I'll meet with the council, and they'll have to decide what to do about replacing Sheriff Stenner."

Leaving the undertaker, Buck rode to the parsonage at the church and knocked on the door. Mrs. Wright informed him that her husband was in his study at the rear of the church, and the deputy made his way through the parsonage to the church. Walking down the aisle between the rows of pews, he found the door marked PASTOR'S STUDY and tapped lightly, calling the preacher's name.

The Reverend Cecil Wright was stunned at the news of Sheriff Stenner's murder, and he repeatedly and nervously ran his hand over his thinning black hair, plastering it to his head. The young lawman asked Wright if he would go with him to the Stenner house when he broke the news to Corrie, adding that Doc Bristol should also be there, considering her poor health.

The minister agreed, and the two men proceeded to the Bristol home. After the physician had been advised of the killing, he accompanied them, taking along his black bag. Along the way they met up with Virgil Orcutt, Mike Hanson, and blacksmith Ken Chitwood.

Mike Hanson observed, "You gentlemen look upset. Has something happened?"

The preacher and the doctor looked at the deputy. His face grim, Buck answered solemnly, "I just found Sheriff Stenner's body in the woods south of town. He was murdered—just like Ron and Vic."

The councilmen were horrified to learn of the sheriff's fate. Recovering slightly, Orcutt asked, "Does Corrie know yet?"

The deputy shook his head. "No. We're on our way now to tell her."

Orcutt's face reflected his shock, and he lamented, "People will be calling this place Widow Valley. Something's got to be done!"

Nodding with agreement, Buck stated, "Our first move

is to have a council meeting. Can you get the rest of the council members together in about an hour, Virgil?"

"Sure. We'll notify the others and meet you at the town hall."

The men parted, and Buck, Wright, and Bristol continued toward the Stenner house. As they walked, the young lawman remarked, "Doc, I'm glad Jenny is still with Corrie. She'll be Corrie's mainstay."

"Jenny's made out of the right stuff for it," Bristol concurred. "As far as I'm concerned, there's never been a young woman like my daughter." After a brief pause he added, "Forgive my fatherly pride."

When the men filed into Corrie Stenner's bedroom, she was sitting up in her bed. Taking one look at their faces, her hand went to her mouth and she gasped, "Something's happened to Bob! What is it? What's happened?"

Buck gave her the bad news, and she began sobbing uncontrollably. The preacher and the physician did their best to comfort her, while Jenny, trembling, flew into the deputy's arms. "How can all this be happening?" she asked frantically.

Leading the young woman out of the room, Buck held her tight and said, "I'm struck numb myself, honey. I just can't figure it out. I know the sheriff has made enemies, as all men who walk behind a badge do, and if it had just been him, I could maybe understand it better. But I'm totally baffled by who'd want to kill all three men."

Though wishing he did not have to leave Jenny, Buck went to meet with the town council. The councilmen were waiting for him when he entered the town hall, and it was obvious that the loss of their sheriff was a real blow to all of them.

Standing before them, the young lawman said, "Gentlemen, we've got a homicidal maniac on our hands, and it appears that he's one of Lander's citizens . . . or at least he lives in the valley. We need help in catching this bloody devil, and to do that, we need an experienced lawman."

Virgil Orcutt spoke up. "You've got a good head on your shoulders, Buck, and I have the utmost confidence in you—as do these other men. I think if you go to work on it, you can flush him out."

Shaking his head, Buck countered, "I appreciate your confidence in me, but I've only worn a badge for less than three years. I'm just not qualified to take on the responsibility of tracking down this killer on my own. But I have a suggestion, and I hope you'll all agree to it."

Orcutt looked at the others, who nodded, then back at Buck. "Okay. We're listening."

"I'd like to see us bring in Wyoming's most famous sheriff for the job—Will Iron. He's got a couple of good deputies over there in Casper who could fill in for him, so there's a good chance he'll come. If you gentlemen have no objections, I'll wire him in the morning. We'll have a town meeting just before the funerals tomorrow, so I can advise the people."

Orcutt again assessed the other councilmen. "Since it's Buck's desire to bring in Iron, fellas, I'm in favor of asking the sheriff to come. Are we all agreed?"

There was immediate concurrence by the others.

"Fine. Send the wire in the morning, Buck."

"I'll do it first thing."

"There's just one more matter of business," the chairman said to the group. "Fremont County needs to have a sheriff, and since the people of the county have authorized us as a body to handle such matters in an emergency like this one, I make the motion that Buck Durand be appointed acting sheriff."

"I second the motion," said Mike Hanson.

"Any questions or discussion?" Orcutt asked the group.

"I have one," Buck stated. "Are you sure a man with my limited experience should even be an acting sheriff?"

"We've watched you work," Hanson remarked. "If it

wasn't for your desire to bring in Will Iron, I'd be for letting *you* handle the job of tracking down the killer."

"You will accept the job of acting sheriff, won't you, Buck?" asked Orcutt.

"Well, yes, sir, but—"

"Good! All in favor, raise your right hand!"

Every hand went up. Orcutt clapped Buck on the back and said, "Be sure to wear the sheriff's badge tomorrow, Buck. We'll miss Bob Stenner real bad, but I'm sure glad we've got *you*!"

Chapter Eight

A heavy sky hung over Lander, and a cold wind whipped across the snow-covered ground as Buck Durand left the telegraph office the next morning and headed toward the undertaking parlor. A tiny bell jingled above the door of Sidney Jager's place as the acting sheriff of Fremont County entered. Hearing a hammer banging loudly from the back room, Buck knew Jager had not heard the bell, and he walked through the reception area, pushing his way through thick damask curtains that hung over the doorway leading to the workroom.

The undertaker was driving down a nail into the pine coffin he was building. At the sight of Buck he paused, nodded, then hit the nail a few more times. He laid down the hammer and his gaze followed the young lawman's to the stack of freshly built coffins stacked in one corner of the room.

The stout Jager folded his hands over his paunch and declared, "Thought I'd get a few made ahead of time. With this killer on the loose, there's a good chance I may be needing more in a hurry."

Buck frowned. "I sure hope not," he responded coolly.

Jager flushed with embarrassment. "Well, me, too

. . . but I figured to be prepared. Even if he doesn't kill anybody else, I'll still need them sometime."

"Guess you're right about that," agreed the sandy-haired Durand with a sigh. "The reason I came by was to tell you that Mrs. Stenner would like to have the sheriff buried today, at the same time the Farnham brothers and Vic Hoffman are buried. Can you arrange it?"

"It'll press me a little," replied Jager. "Not realizing Corrie would want to bury him so quickly, I haven't started on the body yet. But I'll get right on it. I hate to be hasty with it, but I'll get it done."

Buck automatically looked over at the other side of the room where a dark curtain hung from ceiling to floor, and he knew the four bodies lay on slabs behind the curtain. Cold dread settled in his stomach. Who would the killer strike next?

Nodding his thanks to the undertaker, Buck turned and left.

The town meeting was held at nine o'clock, and those few people who had not already heard were stunned to learn that their sheriff had been murdered, though they were relieved that Buck Durand had been appointed acting sheriff. Their fear evident on their faces, the people began to cry out that they wanted Buck for their permanent sheriff, but the young lawman held up his hands for quiet.

"Folks, I feel that I'm too inexperienced to take over in Sheriff Stenner's place, though I deeply appreciate your confidence in me. I promise to do everything in my power to bring the killer to justice, and toward that end I've engaged Sheriff Will Iron from Natrona County to take over this case. I just received a wire from Sheriff Iron, advising me that he'll arrive here within three days."

Murmurs of approval rose from the crowd, though the citizens still voiced their desire for Buck to be their sheriff. Thanking them again, he then informed them,

"The funerals for Sheriff Stenner, the Farnhams, and Vic Hoffman will be held at one o'clock. I'm sure I don't need to tell you that their widows and families will be grateful for your support." After a moment he added, "No matter who's in charge of the investigation, the important thing is that the killing be brought to a halt. And it will! You have my word!"

At one o'clock that afternoon the bell in the tower of the First Methodist Church tolled dolefully as a great crowd gathered at the cemetery, located at the northeast corner of the town. The relentless wind knifed its way over the hillside, chilling everyone to the bone. Four coffins sat in a row, each alongside a yawning, rectangular hole. Looking at the somber boxes and at the weeping women standing near them, several of those assembled echoed Virgil Orcutt's words, calling the place Widow Valley.

There was much crying as the preacher, positioned at the head of the four coffins, conducted the service. Buck Durand stood next to Corrie Stenner, who was flanked on her other side by Jenny Bristol. During the service Buck let his eyes stray to the small, yet ornate, windowless stone building at the center of the graveyard. In that imposing mausoleum, its gray walls stained from rain, sleet, and snow, rested the remains of his mother, who had been interred there over thirteen years before.

The young lawman lost track of what the Reverend Mr. Wright was saying as he thought of the many times his father had forced Errol and him to enter the cold, formidable building while Newt Durand stood and brooded over the dusty coffin resting on a stone platform in the center of the eerie room. Buck remembered that he always came away with chills running up and down his spine and having to pick cobwebs off his clothing. Finally, after Lila Durand had been dead for seven years, Newt stopped going inside the mausoleum, and his sons' torture was ended.

Pulling his gaze away from the crypt, Buck glanced to his right where his father stood between Errol and Ford Loker. Newt was looking straight at him. Their eyes locked for a few seconds, and then the rancher looked away to stare at the snow-covered ground.

When the last prayer had been offered and the service ended, Buck stayed with Corrie Stenner while people filed by to offer their condolences. Corrie hung on to Jenny with both hands, and the acting sheriff worried that the newly widowed woman would not have the strength to endure.

Suddenly Newt Durand broke away from the crowd and walked to the mausoleum with Errol and Loker. Newt stood at the padlocked door, talking to his older son, but Errol shook his head emphatically. Buck was sure that his father wanted to enter the mausoleum and his brother was objecting, for he hated going in there as much as his younger sibling. Newt had often said it should make them feel closer to their mother, but it never did. It only made the two boys shiver with fright and yearn to leave.

After a few minutes of argument the threesome walked away from the somber building. Loker stayed by Newt's side as the wealthy rancher began speaking with some fellow ranchers, while Errol veered off and made a beeline for Jenny.

Ignoring his brother as he drew up, Errol asked, "Jenny, is our dinner date still on for tonight?"

After glancing at Corrie, who was speaking with two other women, Jenny replied, "I really want to talk with you, Errol, but it's going to have to wait until things have settled down for Corrie. She needs me desperately right now, and I'm going to stay with her for a few more days. I'm sorry, Errol, but our dinner will just have to be postponed."

Errol's eyes clouded over. "Oh. Well, all right. I understand. I'll check with you in a couple of days."

The two women paying their respects to Corrie were the last of the mourners, and when they had walked away, Corrie sighed and turned to the young brunette. "We can go home now, Jenny."

Nodding, Jenny put her arm around Corrie's shoulder, and excusing herself to the Durand brothers, she led the grieving widow toward home. Errol glared momentarily at his younger brother before turning his back and walking over to his father and Loker.

Newt Durand's gaze was on Buck. Ending his conversation with the other ranchers, he headed toward his younger son with Errol and Loker at his heels. Clenching his jaw as he approached, Newt pointed to Stenner's grave and grunted, "See there, Buck? That's what happens to a man who wears a badge. You better quit and come back to the ranch before we have to stand over *your* grave."

Drawing in a breath of icy air, the young lawman stated, "Pa, we've been over this whole thing before. Would you like to live in a place that had no law? I mean where there's no man with a badge to protect you?"

"I can take care of myself."

"Maybe so. But how about the rest of the people in this county? Can they?"

Newt pulled the collar of his sheepskin coat tighter around his neck. "I suppose not."

"Then somebody has to wear a badge—and I'm that somebody here."

The older Durand's face hardened. "But why does it have to be you? Why can't it be somebody else?"

"Because I want it to be me, that's why."

Newt stood eyeing the sheriff's badge on his son's coat for a few seconds. Then, without another word, he pivoted and stomped off. Errol gave his brother another glare and followed.

Hanging behind, Loker lingered just long enough to

add with a sneer, "Get out of Errol's way with Jenny. It's him she loves, and you're just messin' things up."

Mindful of the badge on his chest that prevented him from slugging the cowhand, Sheriff Durand muttered, "Mind your own business," and walked away.

The dismal sky was spitting snow when Buck Durand turned onto Main Street and headed toward his office. He was about to unlock the door when he noticed a tall, broad-shouldered man with a weathered face coming toward him on a blue roan. The silver-haired man's left coat sleeve hung empty at his side, and as he reined in, Buck saw the U.S. marshal's badge on his chest.

Turning and stepping to the edge of the boardwalk to meet him, Buck blinked against the snow that blew into his face and said, "Howdy, Marshal."

The big man slid to the ground and looked at the badge on the young lawman's chest. "Howdy. You've got to be Bob Stenner. I declare, they're making sheriffs younger all the time—or is it just that I'm getting old?"

Before Buck could explain about Stenner, the federal man extended his hand and said, "I'm U.S. Marshal Tug Farrell."

As the acting sheriff gripped the big hand, he shook his head, saying, "Bob Stenner is dead, Marshal. I was his deputy. They made me acting sheriff in his—"

"Dead?" Farrell fairly shouted. "Did Swede Andgren get him?"

"Swede Andgren?" repeated Buck with astonishment, remembering well that Andgren had been captured by Sheriff Bob Stenner and the posse a few months previously. Confused, he stated, "He was sent to the state prison at Rawlins in August. He should have been hanged by now."

"He should have," Farrell responded, "but he escaped before they could hang him."

Buck's mind was racing. "Come on into the office, Marshal. I'll stoke up the fire while we talk."

"That'd feel mighty good," Farrell agreed.

As they stepped inside, Buck remarked, "It's an honor to meet you, sir. I've heard a lot about you, Marshal Farrell. Many a story has come through here about your success in tracking down outlaws of every stripe."

"Well, I'd say you might be able to believe about half of those stories," Farrell said with sincere humility. "You didn't tell me your name, son."

"Oh, I'm Buck Durand, sir," he answered, heading for the stove. He described the circumstances of Bob Stenner's death and how he was made acting deputy, then asked, "When did Andgren escape?"

"Eleven days ago. So you don't know who killed Stenner?"

"No, sir. But the day before yesterday, two other men were mysteriously gunned down in the valley, south of town. We've been totally baffled as to who's doing it."

The fire was still smoldering, and the young lawman stoked it with a poker and added wood, then dropped the iron lid. When the room had heated slightly, Farrell removed his hat and then his heavy coat, exposing his left arm in a sling. Seating himself on a straight-backed chair beside the desk, the marshal asked, "Those other two men, were they in the posse that captured Andgren?"

Removing his own coat and hat and hanging them on wall pegs, Buck replied, "Yes, sir. As a matter of fact, they were."

"Other than Stenner, how many men were in the posse?"

Buck pondered the question as he shifted his chair so that he faced the older lawman. Finally he answered, "There were eight men in the posse."

"Were you one of the eight?"

"No, sir. I stayed here to keep watch over the town.

Sheriff Stenner liked to keep one of us here whenever possible."

Farrell leaned his big frame back in the chair and proclaimed, "Well, son, now you know who's doing the killing."

"That's what I'm thinking, Marshal," young Durand responded, relief evident in his voice and on his face. "That is, if Andgren actually came here to do it."

"Oh, he did that, all right," said Farrell. "You see, I was delivering a prisoner at the state prison the very day Andgren escaped. The warden told me that the Swede had repeatedly threatened to escape and head to Lander to kill Stenner and every man in the posse. He was convinced the possemen had gunned down his nephew in cold blood, and he was determined to have his revenge."

Puzzled, Buck asked, "If the warden knew Andgren was coming here to take out his vengeance, why didn't he wire Sheriff Stenner and warn him?"

"He tried, son, but Andgren and the bunch who broke him out had cut the telegraph wires. When he couldn't get a message through, I told him I'd take off after the Swede and his men and do what I could to stop them. I caught up to them a few miles out of Rawlins that first night and had a royal shoot-out. I was able to kill all of them but Andgren, and as you can see, I took a bullet in the fight. I winged the Swede in the leg, but I was down with the slug in my arm, and he got away. Some ranch hands nearby heard the shooting and got me to a doctor, but I had to wait a few days before I could ride again." He sighed, adding, "I was afraid I'd be too late, and as it turns out, I am."

Shaking his head, Buck murmured, "Well, sir, at least there are six members of the posse still alive—and since we now know who's doing the killing, we have a way to keep them alive. One of the men killed the day before yesterday left a message in his own blood, identifying the killer, but the name got smeared. We knew he recognized his killer, so we've naturally been assuming it was someone among us. I'm sure this news is going to make everybody in the valley feel a whole lot safer."

"Well, then, I'm glad my coming can at least do that," commented Farrell.

Leaning forward in his chair, the younger lawman suggested, "Tell you what, Marshal, you sit tight and rest while I round up the town councilmen and bring them here. Once they've heard your story, they'll be as relieved as I am. This will make it easier on Sheriff Will Iron, too."

Buck had already vaulted out of his chair and was donning his hat before Farrell asked, "What's this got to do with the sheriff of Natrona County?"

Putting on his coat, the acting sheriff replied, "We sent for Sheriff Iron to help us track down the killer, knowing he has deputies to spell him. He'll be here in a couple of days."

"I'm glad to hear that," Farrell said with a smile. "I've heard of Iron for years, but I've never met him. It'll be a pleasure to do so."

Buck had the seven members of Lander's town council at his office within ten minutes, and they listened intently as Tug Farrell told them the story of Swede Andgren's threats, of his escape, and of the shoot-out.

When Farrell had finished, Virgil Orcutt and the others were elated to have the mystery solved. Orcutt glanced at Ken Chitwood and sighed, "Oh, what a relief! I'm so happy to know the bloody beast who murdered Ron, Vic, and the sheriff is not one of us!"

Mike Hanson paced back and forth and mused, "The pieces of this puzzle sure have fallen together. Sheriff Stenner led the posse, so he was certainly a prime target for Andgren. Ron Farnham was in the posse, so he was marked, and so was Vic Hoffman. That's why Vic knew his killer. He sure knew Swede Andgren's face."

"Now that we know who to look for," spoke up Buck,

"we need to advise the other posse members, then hold a town meeting and let it be known to everybody."

"I would get to those other possemen first thing," suggested Farrell.

"Three of them are right here," the young lawman told him. Gesturing with his chin, he said, "Virgil, Ken, and Mike all rode after Andgren. The other three are the town's barber, Russ Hendrix; Clarence Iliff, our hostler; and a rancher named Ralph Davis."

"How far out does Davis live?" queried Farrell.

"About four miles," responded Buck. "I'll send somebody out there right away."

"He was at the funerals today," commented Orcutt. "Too bad we didn't know about Andgren then. I'll have my oldest son ride out and tell him, Buck."

"Good. And have Randy inform Ralph that we'll be having a town meeting tonight at seven. I'm sure he'll want to be here." Looking at the other council members, Buck told them, "I'll depend on you gentlemen to help me spread the word about the town meeting."

As the councilmen began to leave, Tug Farrell called after them, "If you gentlemen don't mind, I'll hang around your town and do what I can to help capture Andgren. Maybe the circuit judge will let Lander hang the bloodthirsty killer this time."

"It'd be a pleasure to see him swing by his rotten neck," the big blacksmith growled. "I'll even donate the rope."

"We'll be mighty glad to have you in our midst, Marshal," Orcutt acknowledged.

"Thank you. I'll take a room at the hotel and join in the hunt."

"We'll organize it at the town meeting, Marshal," Buck stated.

"Where do you suppose Andgren is hiding, Buck?" asked Chitwood. "He's surely not stayin' out there in the valley in a gully somewhere . . . not in this weather."

"I'd guess he's holed up somewhere in a barn or shed. Probably in some abandoned building. He couldn't build a fire without drawing attention, but he could stay relatively warm inside four walls without a fire." Buck's face darkened with anger. "Don't worry. We're going to search every possible place. His days are numbered. Now that we know who we're looking for, Swede Andgren's killing spree is over."

The town hall was packed that evening. U.S. Marshal Tug Farrell told the citizenry about Swede Andgren, and when he was finished, he gave a detailed description of the killer for those who had not seen him when he had been tried in August.

Buck Durand then answered questions, calling first on Katie Hanson, wife of the saddler. "Sheriff Durand, now that I know the killer is Swede Andgren and that he's after my husband, I'm more terrified than ever. What can be done to protect Mike?"

The wives of other men in the posse rose to their feet and demanded to know the same thing, but their husbands quickly assured their womenfolk that they would be all right. Other voices joined in, giving opinions on the matter, but the acting sheriff shouted above them, asking for quiet.

When the hubbub had ceased, Buck said, "Andgren has already set a pattern, folks. He seems to want to do his killing when the victim is alone, since this was the case with all three of his victims. What I suggest is that none of you men who served in the posse be alone. Make sure you are always with somebody—and somebody who was not in the posse."

Mike Hanson stood and stated angrily, "I'd rather be out there doing my part to bring that dirty killer to justice, Buck."

The other possemen shouted their agreement.

The young lawman again waited for the noise to die

down before he continued, "I want to assure everyone that we're going to put forth an all-out effort to bring Swede Andgren in, dead or alive. If we haven't caught him by the time Sheriff Will Iron arrives, we'll have Iron's years of experience as a resource. We've already been fortunate enough to have Marshal Farrell join us, so between the two of these seasoned lawmen, Andgren will be stopped, I promise you."

He then called on volunteers to join him in searching every abandoned farmhouse, barn, and shed in the entire valley the following morning. In less than a minute Buck had over seventy men offering their services to scour the valley and hunt down the brutal killer.

With a look of grim determination on his face Buck Durand adjourned the meeting and left the town hall.

Chapter Nine

Within the next two days barns, sheds, and abandoned buildings all over the valley were searched, along with every ravine and gully, but the searchers came up empty. Instructed by acting sheriff Buck Durand to keep trying and stay alert, the volunteers kept up their mission.

The third day, dawn came with a clear sky and crisp air. Clarence Iliff, Lander's fifty-five-year-old hostler, lived with his wife in a small house next to the stable, and as the early light filtered into the cold bedroom, Iliff sat up, yawned, and scratched his thick head of gray hair. Sadie Iliff rolled over and looked at him sleepy eyed. "Time to get up already?" she asked in an indistinct voice.

"Sure is, sweetie," said the hostler, yawning again. "You stay here till I get the fire goin' in the kitchen, and then you can cook me up a hearty breakfast to keep me goin' on our search."

Snuggling deep into the covers, Sadie mumbled, "I'll be up in twenty minutes."

Iliff smiled to himself, climbed out of bed, and hurried into his ice-cold clothes, and by the time he got to his boots, his teeth were chattering. As he was yanking on the

111

second one, Sadie pulled the covers from her face and said, "Clarence, be sure to let Pooch out right away."

"I won't have to, sweetie. I left him in the barn last night."

"You shouldn't have!" she said reproachfully. "It's too cold!"

"Nah," Iliff retorted, standing. "He's got a spot where he nestles in that straw pile. Stays as snug as a bug in a rug. I know he's only a pup, but I'm tired of his leavin' puddles in the kitchen, and—"

"Okay, okay," Sadie cut in. "As long as he's not cold."

Making his way to the kitchen, the hostler removed the lid from the stove and dropped in several pieces of kindling. He then grabbed a small can of kerosene from the windowsill and poured some fuel on the kindling. Just as he was tightening the cap on the can, his dog began barking in the barn, and as Iliff replaced the can on the sill he grumbled, "What's that mutt stirrin' up a fuss about so early in the mornin'?"

He was about to strike a match to light the stove when the dog yelped sharply, and then all was quiet. Concern creased the hostler's brow. He turned his head in the direction of the barn, waiting to hear more from the dog, but when no further sound came, he put the match down and walked to the door, looking out the frost-covered window. Taking his heavy mackinaw from a peg, he put it on but did not bother to button it. He then clapped on his dirty old hat, picked up the single-shot Winchester .44 rifle that leaned in the corner by the door, and stepped outside.

The frigid air was like a slap in the face as Iliff crossed the small yard to the barn. Some of the horses were nickering as he pulled open the big door and peered into the dark interior. "Pooch!" he called. "Here, boy!"

When the dog did not respond, Iliff swung the door open all the way, trying to let in as much light as possible, but most of the barn's interior was still in deep shadow.

Holding the rifle ready, the hostler took two steps and halted, squinting into the corners. The horses were quiet now, looking expectantly at him from their stalls. Iliff whistled and called, "Here, Pooch!" as he moved deeper into the gloom of the building. "Come on, boy! Where are y—"

Clarence Iliff froze in his tracks. Pooch lay stretched out on the floor with blood on his tan coat, just below his jaws. The dog was clearly dead.

Panic prickled the base of the hostler's spine, and his words came out in a fearful wheeze as he waved the rifle back and forth and demanded, "All right, whoever you are, come out immediately! I know you're in here! I'm armed! Come out right now!"

Silence answered him—a silence that seemed to threaten death. Licking his lips, his bulging eyes searching each lurking shadow, Iliff began to backtrack slowly toward the door, his heart pounding in his chest. Suddenly there was a scraping sound off to his right, and he turned to meet it, bringing the rifle to bear. But he was too late. A dark figure made a quick move out of the shadows and rammed a pitchfork into his neck.

The rifle clattered to the hard dirt floor as Iliff instinctively grasped the cold tines of the fork, his eyes fairly popping from their sockets. His thundering heart pumped blood rapidly from the gaping holes, and the sound that was meant to be a scream died in his throat. The killer maintained a solid grasp on the handle of the pitchfork as Iliff fell, clawing at the bloody tines in a desperate struggle to remove them from his throat.

The two men were close enough to the door that the growing light revealed the sinister face of the killer. He stood over Iliff, gripping the handle of the fork so hard that his knuckles were white. When he saw the recognition in the dying man's eyes, a terrible, demonic smile spread slowly on his lips. Then the hostler's eyes glazed over and his struggle ceased.

The killer let go of the fork, leaving it to stand in Clarence Iliff's death grip. Pausing to look down at his victim for a few seconds, he chuckled evilly, then slinked away, closing the barn door behind him.

Sadie Iliff had squeezed out a full half-hour in the warm bed before she rose to don her robe and slippers. Her backless slippers flapped as she walked down the hallway and entered the kitchen, and she was shocked to find the room still icy cold rather than toasty warm as expected. Scowling when she saw that her husband had not even started the fire yet, she noticed that his coat and hat were not on the pegs. This was highly unusual. The hostler had his little routine, and it did not include feeding the horses until after he had eaten his own breakfast. Then she remembered vaguely hearing Pooch barking from the barn before she had dozed off again. The dog always stirred up a fuss whenever he cornered some small varmint in the barn, so her husband must have gone out to see what Pooch had caught this time.

Mumbling to herself, Sadie took up where Iliff had left off at the stove and set it ablaze. While it crackled and popped, she went to the cupboard and took out a can of coffee and measured some into the coffeepot. Rubbing her cold hands together, she held them over the open fire for a few seconds, then dropped three lengths of chopped wood into the stove.

While waiting for the fire to heat up the stove, Sadie made pancake batter and cut off several slabs of bacon, and after that she set the table. Ten minutes later, the stove was hot, the coffee was warming up, and the bacon was beginning to sizzle in the skillet. But before she started the pancakes, she wanted her husband's feet under the table. Going to the door, she opened it and called toward the barn, "Clarence, breakfast is ready!" When no reply came, Sadie shouted louder, "Clarence! Time to eat!"

Sadie figured her husband had decided to go ahead

and feed the horses while he was in the barn. When there was no answer to her third call, she muttered to herself that he could not possibly hear her with the door closed, and she took her coat off its peg, wrapping it around her slender body like a bulky shawl. Stepping into the ever-brightening morning, she hurried to the barn, and as she jerked the door open, she said loudly, "Clarence, breakfast is—"

Her words caught in her throat as the middle-aged woman suddenly felt as though she had been punched in the stomach. Her husband lay flat on his back on the barn floor, gripping the bloody tines of the pitchfork protruding from his throat. It took the stunned woman a brief moment to get her breath, but when she did, a bloodcurdling scream that was repeated over and over pierced the air over Lander.

Within minutes neighbors were gathered at the stable, and acting sheriff Buck Durand was summoned. Several people tried to get Sadie to go back to the house, but sobbing, she insisted on staying close to her husband while Buck removed the pitchfork from Clarence's throat. The young lawman sent one of the neighbors for Dr. John Bristol, then covered the body with a tarp. A few of the women in the crowd wept with fear, saying Swede Andgren was not going to give up until all the men he was after were dead, while others cried that something had to be done to protect the rest of the possemen.

Buck looked around, noting that Virgil Orcutt, Mike Hanson, Russ Hendrix, and Ken Chitwood were all present. So was U.S. Marshal Tug Farrell. Shaking his head with despair, Buck asked, "Marshal, tell me, what's the best way to protect these men?"

"They'll all have to stay somewhere with plenty of protection until that bloody Swede can be caught. As long as they're moving about town, they're vulnerable to Andgren's attack."

The sheriff looked at the four possemen, who were

standing together, and remarked, "You heard the suggestion, gentlemen. Are you willing to hole up till we catch Andgren?"

Orcutt, who owned the town's general store, replied, "I could let my son run the store, but these other men have no one to run their businesses for them."

"That's right," Chitwood confirmed. "If I don't run my business, it won't get run, and I'll be broke in no time. I've got to keep my blacksmith shop going."

"And there's no one to cut hair but me," said Hendrix. "I can't afford to close it down."

"I'm in the same fix," put in Hanson. "I've got a half dozen saddle orders to fill in the next month, plus bridles and some other small leather jobs. I can't stay away from the shop for very long at a time."

Farrell thoughtfully stroked his thick silver mustache. "I can see that the idea of hiding you men in one spot isn't going to work. I could argue that if you get killed, someone else will have to run your businesses, but I understand what you're facing. The only thing to do then is have at least two men guarding you at all times."

Nodding, Buck remarked, "I think that's the best solution, Marshal. How about it, fellas?"

The possemen agreed. From the crowd that had gathered, enough men volunteered to ensure two guards would be with each man twenty-four hours a day, and Buck quickly made out a schedule alloting for eight-hour shifts.

Dr. John Bristol arrived and administered a sedative to Sadie Iliff, then left her in the care of several neighbor women. As he approached the stable to examine the hostler's body, Buck was standing there, telling some of the other men, "I'll ride out to Ralph Davis's ranch as soon as I can and let him know about Clarence's murder. He needs to be alerted so his ranch hands can form a wall of protection around him."

The marshal suggested, "Tell you what, Buck. I'll ride out to Davis's place right now and give him the news.

Since you're losing a number of men to guard duty, you'll have to reorganize your search parties."

The young lawman nodded. "You're right. I wouldn't be able to leave for a while, and the quicker Ralph is alerted, the better."

"Draw me a map, showing me how to find the Davis place, and I'll head out as soon as I can get Dr. Bristol to check my wound and make sure it's healing all right." The marshal glanced at the physician, explaining, "The doctor who treated me said I should have it looked at by today."

Bristol put the tarp back over the corpse and turned away, shaking his head with a look of horrified disgust on his face. Looking up at the tall federal man, he said, "Let's go over to my office, Marshal, and I'll examine that arm."

The two men started walking away, but Buck called, "Stop by the office when you're through, Marshal Farrell, and I'll have that map for you."

At the clinic the physician removed Tug Farrell's bandage and examined the wound. Pronouncing it to be healing nicely, he cleaned it and began to wrap it with a fresh bandage. While he was doing so, Farrell commented, "I've seen some brutal killers in my time, Doctor, but Swede Andgren is definitely among the worst. Poor Iliff. It must have been an awful way to die."

"Horrible," agreed Bristol. "This Swede Andgren is not only a brutal killer, but a very clever one. Have you ever known a man to be so elusive? I mean, he's like a phantom. He shows up just long enough to kill someone, then seems to vanish into thin air."

Easing his arm back into the sling, the strapping lawman said, "Andgren's no phantom, Doctor. He's made out of flesh and blood like the rest of us. You're right when you say he's clever—I'll give him that—but sooner or later, we'll get him. In time even the most dexterous criminal will make a fatal mistake."

Word of Clarence Iliff's death spread through town as U.S. Marshal Tug Farrell, following the map drawn by

Buck Durand, rode toward the Davis ranch. Arriving just after nine o'clock, Farrell was welcomed by the rancher's wife at the door of the large ranch house. She led him down a long hallway and halted before a closed door. Male voices were coming from inside the room. Tapping on the door, she called, "Ralph! You have a visitor"—she smiled—"and I hope you're not in trouble, 'cause he's a United States marshal!"

The door opened and the rancher smiled as he greeted Farrell, shaking his hand. Davis gestured toward a tall, skinny cowhand and said, "Marshal Farrell, meet Lucky Flanagan, my foreman."

As the lawman and the foreman shook hands, Davis remarked, "I hope you're here to give me some good news, Marshal." He put his arm around his wife and continued, "My little honey here hasn't been able to sleep since I told her about that meeting at the town hall the other night when we found out about Swede Andgren . . . and to tell you the truth, I haven't slept so good myself. They catch him?"

"Not yet," replied Farrell, "but I'm afraid I have more bad news. Andgren struck again this morning."

Mrs. Davis's hand went to her mouth, and the rancher stiffened. "Another posse member?" he asked in a strained voice.

"Yes. Clarence Iliff. The Swede rammed him in the throat with a pitchfork."

"Oh, how awful!" exclaimed the woman, gripping her husband's arm.

"Buck Durand has assigned guards to stay with the other four posse members twenty-four hours a day until Andgren is caught. Buck wanted me to tell you that you mustn't go anywhere alone at any time. He wants your men to be constantly vigilant until this thing is over."

"You won't have to worry about that, Marshal," Flanagan assured him. "He'll have a phalanx around him at all times . . . starting immediately."

"Good," Farrell responded. "Keep it that way till you hear differently."

Bidding the rancher and his wife good-bye, the big lawman found his own way out, mounted up, and headed back toward town.

The midmorning sun felt good on Farrell's face as he rode steadily through the sweeping valley. He was nearing a stand of pine and birch trees when suddenly the bark of a rifle shattered the air and a bullet hissed past his ear. As the echo of the gunshot sailed over the treetops and slowly faded out, Farrell dived for the ground. A second shot rang out, and the slug chewed into the snow three feet from him. Hampered somewhat by his wounded arm, the marshal crawled to a shallow gully and rolled over its edge, out of sight. Another shot cut the air and Farrell heard his horse grunt. When he raised his head above the crest of the gully, he saw the animal drop—dead.

Breathing an oath, Farrell pulled his gun and waited for movement among the trees. A sliver of sunlight suddenly glinted off a rifle barrel, and the weapon roared, the bullet humming past the lawman's left ear. Firing back, he sent four shots directly at the spot the shot had come from. Hot lead slammed into the tree bark, but the assailant seemed to be gone. Seconds later Farrell heard racing hooves and then saw a horse and rider emerge from the trees fifty yards away. The horse, a chestnut with four white stockings, bolted in the opposite direction from Farrell, kicking up snow in the process. The marshal stood up and fired his two remaining shots, knowing full well that the gunman was out of range by then.

The federal man went to his dead horse and labored at removing the saddle. Carrying the saddle and bridle, he started walking, finally coming to a ranch, where he flashed his badge and explained to the rancher what had happened. The rancher loaned the lawman a horse so he could ride back to town.

It was almost eleven-thirty when Tug Farrell arrived

back in Lander. He was surprised but pleased to see Buck Durand's horse tied in front of the sheriff's office, and when he stepped into the office, Buck looked up from behind the desk and smiled.

"Did you find Ralph home?"

"Yeah," the big man replied. "He's all set."

"Good."

"I figured you'd be out on the search."

"Not today. I'm expecting Sheriff Will Iron to show up anytime, and I want to be here when he arrives. Besides, Andgren came right into town to do his killing this time, so I thought it might be best if I stay close."

Farrell pulled off his coat, laid it on a nearby chair, then placed his hat on top of it. Sitting down in front of the desk, he said, "I think maybe the Swede's been right here in town all along—right under our noses."

Buck leaned forward. "Do you have some specific reason for believing that?"

"Yeah. He ambushed me when I was riding back from the Davis place. Opened fire with a rifle from a stand of trees. As you can see, he missed me, but he killed my horse. Had to borrow one from a rancher to get back to town."

"You get a look at him?"

"Well, I couldn't see his face, 'cause he was riding away from me and he was a good distance away, too. But it had to be him. I got a good look at his horse, though. He was on a chestnut with four white stockings. Have you seen an animal like that around town?"

"I'm sure there are a couple of them in the valley," replied Buck. "To tell you the truth, if I were to see one on the street, it wouldn't necessarily draw my attention . . . not till now, that is."

"I understand. Well, anyway, I figure Swede's got to be staying right here in town and skulking around unseen. How else would he know I was riding out to the Davis ranch?"

"He could have just spotted you from wherever he's holing up in the valley," the younger lawman suggested. He sighed, muttering, "But I'd bet my best pair of boots that you're dead on target. The dirty rat is hiding right under our noses." Pondering the notion, he added, "The way he lured Clarence Iliff out to the stable this morning suggests he knew the hostler's routine. And the only way he could know what time Clarence would be up so he could kill him and get away clean would be if he was hiding right here in town."

"Seems to me our next move is to search this town thoroughly," the marshal said, running a hand through his thick silver hair.

Standing, the acting sheriff nodded. "I agree. Let's muster as many men as we can right now and get to it."

The young lawman garnered a small group of men, and he and Farrell led a thorough search of every house, barn, shed, and building—including rooftops—in Lander. But they came up with nothing. Frustrated and angry, the sheriff and the marshal returned to Buck's office to await the arrival of Will Iron.

Chapter Ten

The sun was starting to lower when search teams began riding in from the valley to report to Buck Durand. The acting sheriff stood on the boardwalk in front of his office with U.S. Marshal Tug Farrell beside him and listened to one negative response after another as the teams collected in the street. When all the men had returned, Buck told them of Farrell's being ambushed earlier in the day and related the federal man's reasons for believing that Swede Andgren was hiding out somewhere in town. But after describing the thorough search, the young lawman admitted that he was more baffled than ever—and that Andgren was the craftiest of killers.

Just then a lone rider trotted into Lander from the north, and as he came closer, one of the men shouted, "Hey! It's Will Iron!"

Heads swiveled and the famous lawman smiled as he drew rein to a babel of welcoming voices. At the half-century mark in life, Iron's thick dark hair and mustache were now more salt than pepper, and there were deep lines at the corners of his eyes. The tall, slender sheriff was square jawed, rawboned, and as tough as rawhide.

Buck stepped off the boardwalk with Tug Farrell following and approached Iron. Extending his hand as the sheriff dismounted, the young lawman greeted him and introduced himself, and then Buck motioned toward the federal man and said, "Sheriff Iron, this is U.S. Marshal Tug Farrell."

Gripping his contemporary's hand, Iron said, "Tug Farrell! I've heard so much about you over the years. It's a pleasure to finally meet you—though I wish the occasion of my being here was different."

Farrell nodded thoughtfully. "I agree with both sentiments. I'm pleased to meet the famous sheriff of Natrona County, but it's too bad it couldn't be in a social setting."

Iron asked, "May I ask what you're doing in Lander?"

"Well, it sort of ties in with why you're here," replied Farrell.

"Tell you what, Sheriff Iron," interjected Buck, "since we've got the entire town council right here, why don't we all go into the office? We'll tell you the whole story while you warm yourself by the stove."

After acting sheriff Durand dismissed the rest of the searchers, he ushered the council members and the visiting lawmen into his office, while the eight guards assigned to Orcutt, Hanson, Chitwood, and Hendrix waited just outside the door. It was twilight by the time Buck had given Will Iron all the details, bringing him up to the minute. "We all have confidence that your experience will enhance our efforts, Sheriff Iron," the young lawman stated. "Now that you have the complete picture, what else can we do?"

The tall, lanky sheriff rubbed his angular chin and replied, "Let me say first that everything you've done is good. Your thorough search of the town and of the valley was absolutely necessary, but as it hasn't resulted in exposing Andgren's hiding place, it tells us that we're dealing with a very cunning mind. And since we don't know where he's hiding or when he might try to strike again, we need to tighten up even more on security. For one thing, Ralph Davis should come into town." Looking at Farrell, he asked, "Where are you staying, Marshal?"

"At the hotel."

"Well, since that's where I'll be hanging my hat, too, I think that would be the right place for Davis to stay. Let him bring some of his ranch hands to guard him."

Nodding, Buck agreed, "We'll bring him in. Should we do it tonight?"

"I think not. It will be dangerous enough in daylight, so we'd better not try to move Davis to town in the dark. Let's do it in the morning. Just make sure a couple of his men are riding along."

"Okay," Buck concurred. "What else?"

"I think further search would be useless, since you've covered the entire valley. Let's utilize our manpower in a different way now. We should have as many men as possible patrolling the town's borders and streets twenty-four hours a day. I want to catch Andgren, but more than that I want to keep the rest of the potential victims from being killed. The constant patrol will be a show of strength and may serve to keep him from killing again." Looking at Farrell, Iron asked, "Do you agree, Marshal?"

"Sure do," the big man answered. "Andgren seems bent on killing every one of the possemen, so I think the tightening of security, especially using the patrolmen, will eventually flush him out. I was telling Lander's doctor just this morning that given enough time, the most dexterous criminal will make a fatal mistake. Andgren is clearly desperate to avenge his nephew's death, so I'm sure he'll try something in spite of the men on patrol, and that's when we'll get him."

Buck looked at each of the men of the council and asked, "Are you gentlemen in agreement with the sheriff's plan?"

"Since four of us here are the Swede's targets," Virgil Orcutt stated, "I think you'll get a yes vote on Sheriff Iron's plan."

The rest of the councilmen concurred unanimously.

Iron smiled. "Good. Now, let me ask all of you gentlemen a question. Have you considered the possibility that the reason that you're finding Andgren so elusive is because he's not in this alone? That he might have an accomplice?"

Surprise showed on all the other faces in the room. Snapping his fingers, Buck declared, "Now, why didn't I think of that? Sure! Someone we trust could be hiding him. For the life of me, I don't know who it could be . . . but this opens up plenty of possibilities."

Marshal Farrell rubbed the back of his neck. "I should have thought of it, too, Buck. I guess because the last time I saw Andgren he was riding away alone, I just fixed it in my brain that he'd stay that way. Maybe he knows somebody in this area who's willing to help him by giving him shelter."

"And maybe by lending him a horse," put in Iron.

Farrell's face stiffened. "Of course! The chestnut! He wasn't riding a chestnut when I saw him just after he escaped!" He ran his gaze over the group and asked, "Who in this valley owns a chestnut with four white stockings?"

The councilmen eyed each other for a brief moment before Buck replied, "Since you told me about the chestnut the other day, I've been on the lookout for such an animal, and I know of two at this point. Our undertaker, Sidney Jager, owns one. The other belongs to Ford Loker, one of the cowhands on my father's ranch."

Sheriff Iron advised, "Now, let me throw in a word of caution, men. Because these two men own horses like the one ridden by Marshal Farrell's attacker, it doesn't automatically make them suspects. All I can say at this point is that they would bear watching."

Russ Hendrix spoke up. "Seems to me Sid Jager stands to make a lot of money if the killings continue."

Looking annoyed, Charlie Coe admonished the barber, "Hold on, now, Russ. I think your insinuation is unfair. Sid's been here in Lander since he was a kid, and we all know him well. It's no secret he prospers financially with every funeral, but his reputation is impeccable. Why would he get mixed up with a hunk of scum like Swede Andgren? And besides, who else among us would want his job?"

"I'm sorry, Charlie," Hendrix murmured. "I didn't really mean it as an insinuation. I was just thinking out loud."

"My leaning would be more toward that Loker fella, if there are only two to choose from," said the council chairman. "What do you know about him, Buck?"

The young lawman thought for a moment before he answered. He had never liked or trusted Ford Loker— and he liked him less since Loker had been firing up Errol over the situation with Jenny Bristol. Buck's dislike and distrust of the man, however, did not make him an accomplice of Swede Andgren's, and he decided to keep his feelings to himself. Taking a deep breath and letting it out slowly, he finally replied, "Well, Ford's been at the ranch for about five years, and he seems reliable. My pa's happy with the work he does, as is Errol. And Errol and he are best friends." Turning to Iron, Buck explained, "Errol is my older brother."

Iron nodded.

Addressing the group, Buck suggested, "I think the thing to do now is have a meeting with all the men of the town. Let's put Sheriff Iron's plan into action immediately."

At eight o'clock that evening, all the able-bodied men of Lander—except for Sid Jager, who was busy preparing

Clarence Iliff's body for burial—gathered in the town hall. Sheriff Will Iron outlined his plan and had no trouble getting enough men to volunteer as patrolmen—particularly after they were told about the attempt on Tug Farrell's life by the rider of a chestnut horse with four white stockings.

From the back of the room a man called out, "If Andgren's going to start killing at random, none of us are safe anymore."

Farrell shook his head and responded, "No one should let down their guard, sir, but I think he tried to kill me because we fought it out the day he escaped from prison and so he knows I'm after him."

When the meeting was dismissed, several men gathered around the lawmen to talk further. Dr. John Bristol was among them, and after a cursory look at the federal marshal's arm, he pronounced that the dive from his horse had not caused any damage to the wound.

Buck smiled warmly at the man he hoped would soon be his father-in-law and then told Farrell and Iron, "I'll need you two to watch over the town around eight tomorrow morning while I ride out to bring in Ralph Davis and a couple of his men."

"I'll be glad to go for you," said Farrell.

"Or I can do it," offered Iron.

The young lawman shook his head. "I think it should be me this time. Ralph has a bit of a stubborn streak, and he'll probably argue that his men can protect him just as well at the ranch as in town at the hotel. Since I'm the official lawman in the county, my persuasion might hold more authority."

Farrell and Iron agreed and assured him they would be glad to keep an eye on the town.

Shortly before eight o'clock the next morning, U.S. Marshal Tug Farrell and Sheriff Will Iron entered Buck Durand's office. Buck had just finished cleaning his revolver and was punching cartridges into the cylinder, and at the sound of the opening door he looked up, then smiled. "Good morning, gentlemen."

"Good morning," they said.

Tug Farrell looked at his companion for a moment, then said, "Buck, we were talking on the way over here from the hotel, and we don't think you should ride to the Davis ranch alone. Since Swede Andgren seems to know what's going on around here, he might decide to ambush you."

"I don't think so," responded Buck. "He's still concentrating on the possemen. Like you said, he took some shots at you because he knows you're on his trail."

"If he's hanging around close," said Iron, "he knows *you're* after him, too. I think one of us ought to ride along with you."

Shaking his head, the young lawman countered, "I need you both here to watch over things while I'm gone. Don't worry about me. I'll be all right." He then put on his coat and hat and headed out the door.

Buck mounted his horse, and as he backed away from the hitch rail he caught sight of Jenny Bristol about to enter the general store a half block to the north. Seeing him in turn, she smiled and waved to him. He lifted his hat and waved back, then headed south out of town. The sky was clear and the sun was taking the bite out of the air, and Buck was grateful for a break in the cold weather.

Nearing the edge of town, he saw his brother and Ford Loker riding toward him. Loker was on his chestnut gelding with the four white stockings, and suspicions about Loker raced through Buck's head. Could Errol's best friend be tied in some way with Swede Andgren?

The acting sheriff had no desire to stop and talk to the two men, but meeting head-on was going to force it. As they drew abreast and pulled rein, Buck halted his mount. There were no smiles exchanged as Errol eyed his younger brother coldly and said, "We heard about Clarence getting it with a pitchfork. This Andgren fella plays rough, doesn't he?"

"Yeah," replied Buck. "Mighty rough."

"And we heard your U.S. marshal friend got himself ambushed. Andgren do that, too?"

The young lawman could not keep his eyes from going to the chestnut. "Might have been."

"*Might* have been? You're not sure?"

Bringing his gaze back to Errol's face, Buck remarked, "Marshal Farrell thinks it was him, but he couldn't swear to it." He was tempted to describe the horse the ambusher was riding but thought it best to hold his tongue.

His brother remarked, "I wouldn't think you'd be leaving town at all, what with everything going on."

"I wouldn't be, unless it was absolutely necessary. I'm heading to the Flying D to bring Ralph to town for his own safety."

Errol nodded coolly without another word and goaded his mount forward. Buck watched the older Durand and Loker for a moment as they rode away, his gaze focused on the four white stockings of the chestnut. After glaring briefly at the back of the ranch hand's head, the lawman spurred his mount into a trot and continued southward.

Errol Durand and Ford Loker were dismounting at the hitch rail in front of the general store when Jenny Bristol emerged with a small package in her hands. She was obviously surprised to see the two men standing in front of her, and she stopped abruptly and exclaimed, "Oh! Errol . . . Ford. Good morning."

Both men touched their hat brims and smiled at the beautiful young brunette. Errol quickly asked, "How's Corrie doing?"

"Better." She sighed, adding, "Of course, it'll take quite some time before she's at all used to her husband's death, but . . ."

Errol suggested, "Well, since she's doing better, could

we have our dinner date soon? I really do want to talk to you."

Jenny's face went through a few changes. Finally, smiling weakly, she said, "I really want to talk to you, too, Errol. The circumstances aren't exactly as I would have wished, but I suppose now is as good a time as any, if that's okay with you."

A bit flustered at Jenny's sudden willingness to talk, the young rancher started slightly and asked, "Right now? You mean here on the street?"

"Yes," she answered with a nod, clearly eager to get it over with. "I really should get back to Corrie, so how about you walking me to the Stenner house? We can talk on the way."

"Well . . . ah . . . sure. If that's the way you want it."

Loker suggested, "Tell you what, Errol. Since you'll be a while, I'll pick up the things we need in the store and ride on back to the ranch. I need to get back there and take care of something."

"I thought you wanted to have a couple of drinks at the saloon," Errol remarked.

"I'll do that another time," Loker stated with a wave of his hand. Grinning broadly, he added, "You two have a real nice talk now." With that, the ranch hand stepped onto the boardwalk and hurried into the store.

Errol looked down at Jenny. "Here, let me carry that sack for you."

Surrendering the sack, the young woman started down the boardwalk. They had taken only a few steps when she said nervously, "Errol, I'm sorry for the delays that have come up to keep us from getting together. I—"

"Hey, that's all right, Jenny," cut in the tall, muscular man. "It hasn't been your fault."

Jenny shook her head. "No, I really should have just made the time in spite of all that's happened," she said softly.

"Honey, I realize for a good while there you had a

hard time sorting out your feelings between me and my little brother. But in the last couple of months or so, I've been seeing little signs in your eyes . . . and . . . well, sensing something in the way you speak to me. It's been plain to me that you've settled in your heart which one of us it is who you love."

Jenny halted and took hold of Errol's arm. Her face was flushed slightly as she asked, "Have I really been that obvious about it?"

"You sure have," he declared with a smile.

Squeezing his arm, she breathed, "Oh, Errol, I'm so glad you're taking it this way. I've wanted to tell you for several months, but I could never find—"

"Wait a minute," he cut in, frowning. "What do you mean you're glad I'm taking it this way? It's *me* you love, isn't it?"

Jenny's face blanched. Studying Errol's eyes, she replied quietly, "No. I'm in love with Buck. I thought you meant you could see that I wasn't in love with you . . . that I was in love with your brother."

Anger mounted steadily in Errol Durand. His expression hardened and his face darkened. "I was going to ask you to marry me," he growled. "How could you lead me on and then do this to me?"

Blinking, Jenny retorted, "Lead you on? I didn't lead you on! I never told you I loved you! I never said anything to make you think it was you I was falling for. How can you say I led you on?"

Errol's tone was harsh as he answered, "You didn't have to say it! I read it in your eyes and felt it in the way you spoke to me! What made you change your mind?"

"I didn't change my mind! You've been reading and feeling things that weren't there!" Jenny's voice was rising in pitch and in volume, and people on the street were staring.

Errol clutched the grocery sack in one hand and gripped Jenny's elbow with the other. Leading her around the corner to the side street where it was slightly less public, he snapped, "You're lying! It's me you love! I know it! What's my brother done to make you do this to me?"

"You're hurting me, Errol!" she shrieked, jerking her arm loose. "Buck hasn't done anything . . . and I'm not lying!"

Ken Chitwood's blacksmith shop was directly across the street from where Jenny and Errol were standing. Apparently having heard the loud voices, Chitwood stepped outside and called, "Miss Jenny! Do you need my help?"

The brunette burned Errol with a hot look, then looked over at the smithy and said, "No, Mr. Chitwood. I'll be all right. Thank you, though."

Chitwood nodded and waited, keeping his eye on the couple.

Looking back at Errol, Jenny said firmly, "I didn't want this conversation to become a battle."

"Well, what did you expect?" demanded the young rancher. "You lead me to believe that Buck was fading from the picture, and then you hit me in the gut with a battering ram! Look, Jenny, you need to take some time to think this over before you commit yourself to Buck. A future with me is a lot more secure than one with him. With that stupid badge on his chest he'll—"

"I never led you to believe Buck was fading from the picture, Errol Durand!" she countered, her temper rising. "And I don't need any time to think things over! As for committing myself to Buck, it's done! He asked me to marry him, and I accepted his proposal. I'm in love with him and very happy that I will soon be Mrs. Buck Durand. I would like to believe that since we will be in-laws, we could be friends, but that'll be up to you."

"Friends?" he spat. "*Friends!* Oh, sure! My brother steals the woman I love, she cuts my heart out, and we're supposed to be friends!"

Jenny started to speak, but Errol threw the grocery

sack to the ground, splitting it open, then swore vehemently at her and stormed away. Jenny began gathering up the groceries that were scattered on the ground as Ken Chitwood ran to her. Picking up several items, the blacksmith said, "I've got a cloth sack in my shop, Miss Jenny. Come on, I'll get it for you."

Jenny thanked him and followed him across the street, carrying the items in her arms. As she did so she glanced down the street and saw Errol stomp into the Bootjack Saloon.

At the Flying D ranch Buck Durand persuaded Ralph Davis to stay at the town's hotel until the killer was caught, and Davis chose ranch hands Chet Millard and Bud Smith to go along as his bodyguards. Davis had several things to take care of before he could leave the ranch, and it was midafternoon when he kissed his worried wife and rode to Lander, accompanied by Buck, Millard, and Smith.

The four men rode their horses at a walk and discussed the stealthy ways of Swede Andgren. They were about two miles from the ranch when they approached a rock formation jutting up out of the valley floor that sat back some fifty yards from the road. The jumble of rocks, which was partially hidden by snow, covered an area about the size of a large barn, and stubby trees grew out of its cracks.

Buck ran a cautious gaze over the formation as they drew even with it. Noting the acting sheriff's reaction, Davis asked, "See something?"

"Nothing out of the ordinary," responded the sandy-haired lawman, turning to look at the rancher.

He had barely finished speaking when a rifle barked from atop the rock formation, and Ralph Davis grunted and peeled from his saddle. Whipping out his revolver, Buck fired at the spot where a puff of blue-white smoke was hovering in the air, and Millard and Smith immediately followed suit. Bullets chewed rock and ricocheted away angrily, but the rifleman had apparently fled.

The three men slid from their saddles and knelt over Davis. The slug had hit him high in the chest, but he was still breathing. Standing and looking toward the rock formation, the young lawman ordered, "You guys wrap his wound with something and get him to Doc Bristol as fast as you can. I'm going after that dirty buzzard."

Vaulting back into the saddle, Buck bolted toward the rock formation, gun ready. He picked his way carefully over the rocks and reached the back side in time to see a rider on a chestnut horse with four white stockings galloping across the valley toward the mountains. The man was already some five hundred yards ahead, pushing the chestnut for all it was worth, making it impossible to determine his shape or size.

Buck spurred his mount and took off in hot pursuit. The rider looked back from time to time, lashing the chestnut with the reins, and maintained his lead. As the killer neared the foothills, the lawman swore, for if the killer got into the timber just beyond the foothills, he would get away. Buck urged his horse on, hoping to gain ground, but soon the elusive man was bounding over the foothills, heading for high country.

By the time Buck's puffing horse brought him to the edge of the timber, the rider was out of sight and the acting Sheriff soon lost the trail in the dense underbrush. Cursing, he headed back to town.

When Buck galloped into Lander, a large crowd of people was gathered at the cemetery, burying Clarence Iliff. The young lawman felt bad that he had not been in town for the funeral and could not even spare the time to attend the last few moments of the ceremony, but his priority was toward the living, and he had to check on Ralph Davis at Doc Bristol's office. Riding up Main Street, he thought of Sadie Iliff standing beside her husband's coffin, and his heart went out to the latest woman to join the grieving ranks of the valley's new widows. He prayed that Mrs. Davis would be spared such grief.

Swede Andgren's face as he had remembered it from the trial was engraved on Buck's mind like a photograph. *I'll get you, Andgren,* he thought. *It may be the last thing I do, but I'll get you!*

Reaching the clinic, Buck dismounted beside Ralph Davis's horse and noted the vast amount of blood on the saddle. When he stepped into John Bristol's office, Millard and Smith were in the waiting room, and they both stood when he entered. "Did you catch him?" Smith asked urgently.

"No," Buck replied glumly. "He got to the high timber too far ahead of me. How's Ralph?"

"Still hangin' on," said Smith. "Doc Bristol's not here. He's out somewhere deliverin' some ranch woman's baby. His daughter's workin' on the boss."

"Oh?" the young lawman said, walking to the closed door of the examining room. Rapping lightly, he called, "Jenny, it's Buck. May I come in?"

"Yes," came the muffled response.

He entered, closed the door, and looked across the room. Ralph Davis lay on the operating table, unconscious, with a large bandage over his wound, and Jenny was at the washstand removing the blood from her hands. Giving Buck a concerned look, she queried, "Did you catch Andgren?"

"No. He had too great a start on me and I lost him." Taking a couple of steps, he asked, "How's Ralph doing?"

"Not very well, I'm afraid," Jenny replied, picking up a towel and drying her hands. "Father's out at the O'Brien ranch, and I had to go ahead and remove the bullet by myself or Mr. Davis would certainly have died. As it is, he's lost so much blood, I'm not sure he'll make it. He's critical, to say the least."

The young brunette walked over to Buck and said softly, "I spoke with Errol earlier. You probably saw him and Ford Loker come into town. Anyway, I couldn't wait any longer. I had to let him know about us."

"You told him in front of Loker?"

"No. Knowing Errol and I were going to talk seriously, he told Errol he would meet him back at the ranch. I told your brother about us while he was walking me to Corrie's house."

"How'd he take it?"

"Not well at all. As a matter of fact he was furious and said some pretty harsh things. He then went to the Bootjack Saloon. His horse was still in front of the saloon when I came here from Corrie's to take care of Mr. Davis."

"I'm sorry he took it that way," Buck said ruefully.

Jenny was quiet for a moment, then remarked, "Buck, Mr. Davis's ranch hands said the man who shot him was on a chestnut horse with four white stockings.

"I . . . well, I hate to have to say this, but your father's ranch and the Davis place are in the same direction from town. Ford seemed almost eager to head back to the ranch, and he rides a chestnut with four white stockings, as you know."

"Yeah," the handsome young lawman muttered, taking hold of Jenny's upper arms and looking into her eyes. "I've been thinking the same thing. It turns my stomach, but I think Loker may somehow be linked with Swede Andgren and is helping him do the killing."

"If it's true," Jenny said shakily, "Errol's in for another hard blow. Ford's his best friend."

"I've got to find out if it's true," Buck said, pulling the young woman close to him. "So I'm going out to the Box D right now."

Bending, Buck kissed Jenny tenderly on the lips, and there were tears in her eyes when he released her. With a tremulous voice she said, "Oh, Buck, be careful. If Loker *is* in cahoots with Andgren and you close in on him, he'll probably try to kill you."

"I'll be careful, darling," he replied softly "I want this nightmare to be over with because you and I have a wedding to plan."

He kissed her again, then headed for his father's ranch.

Chapter Eleven

"You *what*?" blared Newt Durand, glaring hotly at his son.

Buck Durand and his father were standing on the front porch of the ranch house, where Newt had met him when he dismounted. The sun was setting over the nearby Wind River mountains, and its deep-red glare matched the color of the older man's face.

Buck squared his shoulders. "I said I'm going to question Ford Loker as to his whereabouts this afternoon at the time Ralph Davis was shot from ambush."

The rancher shook his head. "Have you lost your mind, boy? No man that works for this outfit would do a thing like that! Why do you suspect Ford?"

"Because the gunman I chased into the mountains rode a chestnut with four white stockings. Yesterday Marshal Farrell was ambushed by a man on a horse of the same description. Now, I didn't have to talk to you about this. I could have just gone to the bunkhouse. But I thought you should know what's going on."

Newt kept his voice low but spoke with an intensity that revealed his fury. "You get on your horse and ride, mister! I will not allow you to put one of my men into a corner with your questions!"

Shaking his head, his son stated, "You don't understand, Pa. I'm not asking for your permission to question Loker. I merely stopped at the house to advise you that I came here to talk to him and why."

A nerve was pulsing in the wealthy rancher's left temple. "Where do you get the gall to ride onto my property and tell me what you're going to do?"

"It's not gall, Pa," the younger Durand replied calmly. "It's authority." Indicating the badge on his chest, he continued, "And this is my authority. Don't try to stop me."

Before Newt could respond, his son turned and stepped off the porch, heading for the bunkhouse. Hurrying alongside the younger man, the rancher raged, "That stinking badge is going to get you in deep trouble one of these days, Buck!"

Ignoring him, Buck walked into the bunkhouse and gazed around the room at the ranch hands until he located Ford Loker, who was stretched out on his bed. Striding to Loker's bed, the young lawman stood over him and snapped, "I've got a question for you."

The cowhand sat up, looked at Newt as he reached his son's side, then stood and faced the acting sheriff. "What's your question?"

"Shortly after you left my brother in Lander this morning, you rode out of town. Where were you at two-thirty this afternoon?"

Loker's chin jutted stubbornly. In an icy voice he grunted, "Why do you want to know?"

Newt stepped between them. "Ford, you don't have to answer him. This kind of balderdash is a downright insult!"

Buck eyed his father and stated, "I'm here on official business as sheriff of Fremont County, so don't get in my way. I've got a bloody killer to bring to justice, and I intend to do it."

The other ranch hands looked first at each other, then

at Loker, who demanded of his interrogator, "Are you accusin' me of bein' the killer who's makin' widows all over this valley?"

"I'm not accusing you of anything at the moment," the young lawman replied, attempting to keep his voice level. "I'm just asking you where you were this afternoon at two-thirty."

"I was out ridin'."

"By yourself?"

"By myself. There a law against that?"

"No, but there's a law against shooting a man down from ambush."

Loker's brow furrowed. "Who was shot from ambush?"

"Ralph Davis. I was with him, and so were two of his men. The ambusher rode away on a chestnut with four white stockings."

There was a moment of stunned silence, which Loker broke by stating flatly, "Oh, so because I ride a chestnut that has four white stockin's, that makes me the guy who shot Davis."

"I said I'm not accusing you, Ford. But you must admit there aren't too many chestnuts in the valley that look like yours."

"That still don't make me guilty."

Clearly astonished at the news, Newt asked, "Is Ralph dead?"

Buck sighed. "He was still alive when I left town, but he's critical."

"Well, whether he lives or dies," said Loker, "you ain't pinnin' it on me."

Buck looked him straight in the eye and rasped, "If you didn't do it, I won't pin it on you. Where's your rifle?"

"Right here next to my bed. Why?"

"Let me see it."

Loker regarded the lawman obstinately, but as it was obvious from the ominous look on the young lawman's face that the cowhand would be in serious trouble if he did not comply, he wordlessly turned and reached for the gun.

While Loker was getting the rifle, Newt asked his son, "Is your brother still in town?"

"As far as I know."

"What's he doing there?"

"I think he's getting drunk. He's been at the Bootjack all day."

"Why would he do that?"

"He's upset because Jenny told him this morning that she's going to marry me."

Every man in the bunkhouse was clearly shocked, and it was evident that Errol had convinced them that he and Jenny were about to become engaged.

Newt's mouth hung open, but Buck turned from him and took the rifle from Ford Loker's hand. He sniffed it at the chamber and, looking suspiciously at the cowhand, remarked, "This gun's been fired quite recently. Today, for sure."

"I took a couple of shots at a coyote while I was out ridin'," Loker said defensively.

Handing the rifle back to its owner, the young lawman stated, "I can't arrest you just on this evidence, but be assured I'm keeping a close watch on you."

Loker bristled, and his face flushed with anger. "I resent this!" he spat. "I don't like bein' a suspect just 'cause of the way my horse is marked and 'cause I shot at a varmint!"

"Your resentment doesn't bother me," Buck retorted. "You *are* a suspect."

Newt Durand suddenly began shaking his fist at his son as his own anger increased to rage. "That's it, Buck!" he bellowed. "You just lost the remainder of your inheritance! I'm disowning you—and Errol will get *everything* when I die!"

Buck ignored his father and warned Loker, "Remember what I said. I'm keeping a close watch on you." With that, he turned and walked out of the bunkhouse.

Fuming, Newt stomped to the door and watched

through the gathering twilight as his younger son mounted and rode away. He then turned and pointed at four cowhands, ordering, "You men go into town after supper and bring Errol home from the saloon."

Entering Lander just after darkness had fallen, Buck Durand went home, washed up, and headed for the doctor's office. John Bristol was back and sadly informed Buck that Ralph Davis had died from loss of blood. The preacher and another townsman had gone out to break the news to Mrs. Davis.

Not having eaten since an early breakfast, Buck headed for the Eagle's Nest Café for supper, noting as he passed the saloon that his brother's horse was still tied out front. When he reached the restaurant and went inside, he saw U.S. Marshal Tug Farrell and Sheriff Will Iron just sitting down at a table. They spotted him and asked him to join them.

While the three lawmen ate, they discussed the latest events. The young lawman was finishing the story of what had happened at his father's ranch when an elderly man bolted through the door, looked around for a moment, then threaded his way to where Buck sat and said excitedly, "Sheriff, there's trouble over at the Bootjack! Errol's beating Webb Tolleston to a pulp!"

Leaping from his chair, Buck dashed out the door, and seconds later he raced into the saloon with the older lawmen trailing a few yards behind. He found his muscular brother standing over the slender, middle-aged Tolleston, who lay on the floor in a daze with his face battered and his lower lip split open. The dozen or so other patrons stood around with the bartender in a half circle, and Farrell and Iron slipped in among them.

Buck gave his brother a cold stare, then knelt beside Tolleston, a cowhand on a local ranch. Scrutinizing the damage, he looked at the group and instructed, "Somebody go get Doc Bristol."

As a man hurried out the door the young lawman stood up and faced his sibling. "What happened here?" he snapped.

"He's got a big mouth!" growled Errol, who was swaying on his feet, his eyes bloodshot and watery.

"Errol started it, Buck," one of the witnesses declared. "All Webb did was ask how things were goin' between him and Jenny Bristol, and your brother acted like a madman."

A number of other men concurred with the assessment.

Regarding Errol with a stare as hard as agate, Buck upbraided his brother. "You drunken fool! You had no cause to attack Webb!" With a look of disgust he added, "If he wants to press charges, you're going to feel the discomfort of one of my jail cells."

His hatred for his sibling obvious, Errol headed for the door on less-than-steady legs, calling his rival a few choice names over his shoulder.

"Hold it right there!" Buck shouted, hurrying after him. "You're not going anywhere until Doc Bristol arrives! When Webb's head clears, we'll see whether I jail you or not!"

Errol swore, shoved his brother out of the way, and bellowed, "You're not telling me what to do!" He then reached for the batwing doors.

The acting sheriff muttered under his breath, "I didn't want to have to do this," and he spun Errol around by the shoulder, then hurled a fist into his jaw. The blow slammed the drunken young rancher into the wall, and he fell to the floor, shaking his head.

Standing over him, Buck nodded toward the nearest table and ordered, "Now, sit down like I said!"

Grudgingly, Errol struggled to his feet and made his way to the table and slumped in a chair.

Dr. John Bristol arrived and examined Webb Tolleston, who was now seated in a chair on the opposite end of the room from his assailant. After a brief examination Bristol announced that no teeth were loosened, and that the split lip would not need stitches. While the doctor administered salve to Tolleston's lip, Buck asked the injured cowhand if he wanted to press charges. Being an understanding man, Tolleston said he did not, if Errol would pay for Bristol's services.

Reluctantly Errol forked over the amount, and the physician stuffed the money in his pocket, closed up his black bag, and left. Two men assisted Tolleston to his horse, and after he had left, Buck told his brother, "You're lucky Webb didn't press charges. I hope you won't do anything so stupid again."

Swearing vehemently at his sibling, Errol staggered out of the saloon.

Mike Hanson and Ken Chitwood were among the patrons, and as men lined up at the bar for drinks, Hanson and Chitwood sat down at a table with the three lawmen. They discussed Ralph Davis's death, and Buck told the councilmen and his colleagues about his talk with Ford Loker at the Box D—not mentioning that his father had disinherited him.

After a few minutes Buck stood up and said, "If you gentlemen will excuse me, there's a certain beautiful young lady that I want to visit. I'll see you all in the morning."

Striding quickly to the batwing doors, the acting sheriff stepped outside and found the street virtually deserted, though Errol's horse was still tied to the hitch rail. Puzzled, he looked around, but his brother was nowhere to be seen. "Now, that's odd," he mumbled. "Where could he have—"

Suddenly he heard a moaning sound coming from the narrow passageway between the saloon and the hardware store. Rushing there, he found Errol sprawled facedown on the ground, just off the boardwalk. The small bit of light from the streetlamps that penetrated the deep shadows allowed him to see a bloody length of two-by-four lying across his brother's back. The back of Errol's head was bleeding profusely, and he was barely conscious.

Buck picked up the two-by-four with one hand and was about to lift Errol so he could take him to the doctor when four ranch hands from the Box D hauled up. They spotted Buck standing over Errol with the length of wood in his hand, and just as Farrell, Iron, Hanson, and Chitwood were coming out of the saloon, one of the ranch hands shouted, "Hey! Buck just bashed Errol with a club!"

Buck looked down at the bloody two-by-four in his hand, then up at the young cowpoke who had spoken. "That's ridiculous! I did nothing of the kind," Buck retorted with a note of irritation in his voice. "Somebody go get Doc Bristol. Errol's hurt bad."

Hanson volunteered to go and hurried off.

The Box D men dismounted and approached Buck and his fallen brother. Farrell and Iron stepped beside their young colleague as Buck dropped the two-by-four and knelt beside his sibling, whose eyes were fluttering. Brushing the wounded man's hair from his eyes, Buck asked, "Errol, who hit you?"

"Don't deny it, Buck," Errol mumbled. "You did it."

One of the Box D men immediately said to the older lawmen, "You heard it! Buck's the one who did it! Probably if we hadn't arrived when we did, he'd have killed him!"

"That's preposterous!" Buck protested. "I had just found him when you rode up!"

The Box D man snorted and exclaimed, "Hogwash! Buck was told by his dad just a short while ago that he was being disinherited and that Errol was going to get everything. Looks to me like Buck was nursing a real grudge." He stared at Farrell and Iron, commanding, "Put Buck under arrest for attempted murder!"

A sizable crowd had collected, and there was a great deal of confusion as many of the townsmen objected, arguing that if the acting sheriff said he had not attacked his brother, then he had not. The Box D men argued back that by Errol's own words, Buck was guilty.

Will Iron knelt beside Errol and said earnestly, "These are mighty serious charges you've hurled at your brother. Are you sure it was Buck who hit you?"

"I'm sure," answered Errol, his words hoarse.

Dr. Bristol arrived on the run and asked the men to carry Errol out into the light. After the young rancher was stretched out on the boardwalk directly under a streetlamp, Bristol turned him on his side and examined the blood-soaked area on the back of his head.

One of the Box D men demanded, "Well, Sheriff Iron, are you gonna arrest Buck, or do you lawmen stick so close together that no matter what any of you do, it ain't wrong?"

Dr. Bristol looked up and asked, "Am I hearing right? Buck's being accused of doing this?"

"Errol *said* he did it, Doc!" spoke up one of the townsmen.

"I did not do it," Buck said evenly. "He was like this when I found him."

Bristol eased Errol once again onto his back, and the wounded man licked his lips and said weakly, "It was Buck who . . . hit . . ." The words trailed off, and Errol Durand's body went limp, his head lolling to the side.

The physician felt for a neck pulse, and when he could not find one, he quickly took his stethoscope from the black bag and listened for a heartbeat. There was none. Rising to his feet, he breathed, "He's gone. His skull was cracked."

Buck winced, feeling both great sadness and anger. Looking around, he said, "I didn't do it. Errol was mistaken."

Doc Bristol placed his stethoscope in the bag and nodded his agreement. "He *was* hit in the back of the head, after all, so how could he have seen who hit him?"

"Exactly. He didn't," Buck replied. "Errol assumed it was me because he and I have been having some . . . well, disagreements."

"You sure have!" declared one of the townsmen. "We saw one of your disagreements a few minutes ago in the saloon. You punched your brother pretty hard in there."

"He had to!" another man insisted, going to the young lawman's defense. "You saw what happened!"

Voices were raised in argument, but it was clearly evident that most of the townsmen present believed that Buck was telling the truth. When everyone quieted down, one of the Box D ranch hands looked at Farrell and Iron and stated flatly, "It doesn't matter what anybody thinks. Buck's been incriminated by the testimony of a dying man—which means somehow Errol *did* see Buck before he struck him."

"Sure!" put in one of the townsmen, his voice filled with irony. "Errol saw him standin' there holdin' that club, then turned his back so's Buck could clobber him. Don't be an idiot!"

Ignoring the man, the cowpoke insisted that Buck had to be arrested for murder.

Will Iron sighed and said, "Buck, the law we serve protects the innocent. That's why we have courts and trials. I don't believe you did your brother in, but you'll have to surrender your gun and badge and be locked up until the circuit judge comes around. You can be sure we'll investigate further, and we'll present all findings in court. Since I have no authority in Fremont County, the United States marshal present will have to arrest you."

Buck Durand was stunned as Tug Farrell held out his hand, palm open, and muttered, "Sorry, Buck."

After handing over his gun to the lawman, Buck removed his badge. As he gave it to Farrell, he said bitterly, "It's Swede Andgren, Marshal. He's hiding somewhere in this town, and he just murdered my brother."

One of the ranch hands asked, "Why should Andgren kill Errol? He wasn't in the posse."

"Andgren's a madman!" Buck retorted heatedly. "He's starting to kill at random!"

Sidney Jager was called to pick up the body, and the Box D men headed for the ranch to tell Newt Durand that his older son had been murdered—and his younger son had been arrested for the crime.

Sickened, Buck was escorted to the jail and ushered into a cell. "This is crazy!" he said to Farrell and Iron as the cell door clanged shut. "It's almost as though Andgren set it up to get me out of the way!"

"It has a stink to it, all right," agreed Farrell. "But let's face it, there was no way Andgren could've known that you would be the one to come out of the saloon and find Errol."

Rubbing his face, Buck sighed. "Yeah, you're right," he said glumly. He clenched his fists and groaned, "This is terrible! I can't stay in here! I've got to be out there, hunting that butcher down! I've—"

He stopped speaking when he heard the office door opening and closing, followed by light, rapid footsteps coming toward the cell area. Presently, Jenny Bristol appeared, her face ashen. She stopped for an instant when she saw Buck standing behind the bars, then rushed to him, reaching through the bars to take his hands. "Father just told me what happened, and it's an outrage! I'm so sorry about Errol, but for him to implicate you as his assailant is utterly insane!"

Gripping her hands, Buck drew close to the bars and said, "I know, honey, but it looks like I'm stuck here till the court can clear me."

Tears ran down her cheeks. "Oh, Buck, this is awful! That Andgren must be caught!" Looking at Farrell and Iron, she cried, "What are you going to do?"

"Everything we can, miss," replied Iron. "But I must admit, we're dealing with the most cunning criminal I've ever encountered."

Nodding his agreement, Farrell added, "All I can say is what I said before: One of these days Andgren will make a mistake, and when he does, we'll get him."

*   *   *

The next morning Tug Farrell and Will Iron brought Buck his breakfast and were talking to him while he ate when Newt Durand stormed into the cell area. Brushing past the two lawmen as if they did not exist, he glared at Buck with blazing eyes and screamed, "You killer! You clubbed your own brother to death because he was getting all the inheritance!" He spewed out curses at his younger son with all the fury of a volcano.

The burning words cut Buck to the quick, and he flinched as though he had physically been assaulted. Pale, he said softly, "Pa, I—"

"Don't you *pa* me!" boomed Newt. "I have no son who would murder his own brother! I hate your guts!"

"I didn't kill Errol," the young lawman insisted. "You've got to believe me."

"I don't believe you! Errol told everybody there that you clubbed him! Don't lie to me! What would your poor mother say if she were alive to see this?"

"She would say that *she* believed me," replied Buck. "She would know that I would never kill Errol."

But Newt Durand refused to listen to his son's explanation. So angry that he looked as though he would explode, he whirled and stomped out. When the outer door slammed, Buck said, "Marshal Farrell, you've got to let me out so I can find Andgren and clear myself."

Suddenly the outside door opened again and footsteps sounded, followed by a high-pitched male voice asking, "Marshall Farrell, are you here?"

"That's Henry Stone," said Buck. "He's our telegrapher."

Farrell nodded and turned toward the office. "Back here!"

Henry Stone was in his late sixties and quite frail looking. Stepping into the cell area, his bony body halted when he saw the three men. Looking at Buck, he said, "I heard what happened, son. Sorry about your brother. But

I'm sure it'll all be straightened out when the judge comes to town." Then he approached Farrell, extended a yellow sheet of paper, and said, "The wire service has just been restored tween here and Rawlins, Marshal. This telegram's for you—and it's a shocker!"

Farrell took the paper and began reading. Suddenly all the blood seemed to seep out of his face, and deep lines furrowed his brow. When he had finished reading, the U.S. marshal ran his gaze between Buck and Iron and said in a strained voice, "It's from Warden Ed Childers at the state prison. He says that Swede Andgren's body was found in an abandoned shack about thirty miles north of Rawlins a few days after the prison break, still dressed in prison grays. He had bled to death from the slug I put in his leg."

The cell area was as silent as a tomb as the implication of the news sank in. Stunned, Buck finally broke the silence by saying, "Then . . . then the killer really is someone among us. We've got to tell the people."

Farrell and Iron went to Virgil Orcutt and showed him the telegram. A town meeting was called, and everyone was told the news. Terror washed over the crowd as they realized that someone they all knew was the killer.

A number of the citizens demanded that Buck Durand be released from the jail, and the council members all declared that they, too, believed Buck to be innocent and asked Farrell to let him out. But the marshal explained that because Errol Durand had implicated his brother as his assailant, Buck would have to be cleared by a court of law before he could be released. The federal man added that he and Sheriff Will Iron would remain in Lander until the killer was brought to justice. Once he had been caught, Farrell was sure it would be proven that the same man who had been doing the killing had murdered Errol. The young lawman would be exonerated and free once again to serve as acting sheriff of Fremont County.

Chapter Twelve

T he bell in the church tower tolled out its mournful peal
through the clear, morning air as people from all over the
valley gathered in the cemetery for the burials of Ralph
Davis and Errol Durand. Buck Durand had been allowed
to attend his brother's funeral, and Jenny Bristol was at his
side as he emerged from the sheriff's office in handcuffs.
Tug Farrell and Will Iron flanked the couple as they
walked through town.

When they reached the cemetery, Newt Durand and
all of his nearly two dozen ranch hands were standing near
Errol's coffin. Buck felt the hard eyes of his father and the
Box D men on him as he drew up with Jenny and joined
the crowd of mourners.

When the doleful bell stopped ringing in town, the
preacher began the service with prayer. While the Reverend Cecil Wright read Scripture and made comforting
comments, Buck's gaze strayed to the formidable mausoleum that housed his mother's body. Even in the bright
sunlight it was dismal, and a chill ran down his spine as he
pictured its cold, dusty, cobwebbed interior. Recalling his
mother, who had been so vibrant and loving, he thought,
*Mom, how could things get so messed up? I wish you were
here to convince Pa of my innocence.*

Buck looked over at his father and the ranch hands, and he found that Newt and at least half of his men were glaring at him, clearly believing he had murdered Errol. Ford Loker's eyes were particularly cold. Averting his eyes and looking at the coffin that held his brother, the young lawman found his vision obscured by tears as memories of the happy childhood they had shared crowded into his mind.

When the preacher had concluded the service, the mourners expressed their sympathies to Mrs. Davis, Newt Durand, and Buck. Every person who spoke with the younger Durand expressed their faith in him, assuring him that soon he would be exonerated.

Will Iron was about to return his prisoner to the jail when Newt walked over to Buck and fixed him with hate-filled eyes. His voice trembled with rage as he told his son, "I hope you hang!"

Squeezing Buck's arm comfortingly, Jenny's voice quivered as she murmured, "Mr. Durand, you'll soon learn how wrong you are about your son."

Newt's hard eyes studied her finely chiseled features for a long moment; then without a word he walked away.

Seeing the deep hurt in Buck's face, she wrapped her arms around him, whispering, "When Errol's killer is caught and you're cleared, your father will come to you, darling."

Buck did not comment as he held her tightly. Finally he looked down at her, kissed the tip of her nose, and told her quietly, "I love you so much, Jenny. Your support and belief in me is what's going to help me get through this nightmare."

After telling the young lawman that she would visit him that evening, Jenny headed to Corrie Stenner's house. Tug Farrell and Will Iron escorted Buck back to the jail and found a crowd waiting in front of the office. At their approach, people starting shouting at the lawmen, asking how they could protect themselves with a vicious killer at large among them. Tug Farrell replied that the patrolmen would continue to ride the perimeter of the town and patrol the streets, adding that all the men and women should arm themselves and stay alert.

Sheriff Iron commented that it would no longer be necessary for the possemen to have special guards, since it was not Swede Andgren doing the killing. But he then suggested that *none* of the townspeople be alone in their homes or on the streets if at all possible. Even though the killer had so far murdered only men, they must not assume that the women and children were safe.

When night came, Jenny was at her father's office doing some bookwork for him while he administered sedatives to terrified women. When the young brunette had finished, she told her father she was going to visit Buck at the jail and would have one of the patrolmen escort her there.

Stepping out on the street past the waiting husbands, Jenny gazed up and down the dimly lit street until she spotted one of the men on patrol. It was J. C. Dooley, a stout man in his midfifties who owned the Lander Feed and Grain Company. Waving a hand, she called to him, and Dooley hurried to her.

"Good evening, Jenny. Is there something I can do for you?" he asked.

"I need an escort down to the jail, Mr. Dooley," she replied. "I know it's only a block and a half, but Father asked me not to go anywhere unaccompanied, and he's busy with patients."

"A wise suggestion on your father's part—and a wise decision on yours," Dooley stated, giving her his arm. When they arrived at the door of the sheriff's office, a lamp was burning inside and they could see Will Iron through the window. The patrolman asked, "Would you like me to escort you home after you've visited Buck?"

"That would be very kind of you," Jenny answered. "Give me a half hour, if you don't mind."

"See you then," he promised and continued down the street.

Stepping inside, she greeted the lawman and told him, "I'd like to visit with Buck for a half hour, if that's okay, Sheriff Iron."

"That'll be fine," Iron told her. "Tell you what. I was just going out to do some patrolling, and Marshal Farrell is already out there, so I'll give you one of the spare keys. Lock yourself in after I leave, and lock the door behind you when you go. Give the key to the nearest patrolman. Is someone seeing you home?"

"Yes, sir. The patrolman who walked me here is coming back for me."

Nodding, Iron left.

Jenny locked the door and rushed to the cell area, kissing Buck through the bars. She tried to encourage him, and they held hands as they talked, speaking of their love for each other.

Patrolling alone on a side street under a pale moon hanging in the clear Wyoming sky, U.S. Marshal Tug Farrell pulled out his pocket watch to check the time. By the dim light he was barely able to read that it was ten o'clock. He decided to head back to the business district where he would patrol a section of Main Street, then return to his hotel.

He was looking conscientiously back and forth on both sides of the street when a small dog began yapping at him from the porch of a house. Startled by the abrupt sound, he automatically reached for the butt of his revolver. Checking himself, he mumbled softly to the little animal as it kept barking, "Hey, fella. You almost went to doggie heaven."

The dog continued barking as Farrell walked toward the next house. Suddenly he was hit hard from behind and fell unconscious to the ground. The shadowed figure dropped the tree limb he had used as a club, then dragged the marshal through the dark streets, cautiously watching for patrolmen as he headed for the cemetery.

Twice the assailant had to pull the federal man's heavy, limp form into bushes to avoid being seen. Reaching the cemetery, he waited for a mounted patrolman to round the outside corner and pass from view. Knowing another one would be along shortly, he quickly dragged Farrell among the tombstones toward the mausoleum housing Lila Durand's coffin. He was almost there when above the sound of his labored breathing and the swish of Farrell's body on the crusty snow, he heard hoofbeats. Another patrolman was making his way along the outside edge of the cemetery. The dark figure quickly ducked down, waiting for the rider to pass.

Tug Farrell began to moan and roll his head, and the man shot a glance at the mounted patrolman, impatient and anxious for him to hurry along. The federal man was coming to rapidly, and his moans were increasing in volume. Knowing further delay would mean exposure, the shadowed figure rose to his knees and punched Farrell as hard as he could on the jaw. The marshal slumped and lay motionless again.

The valley's mysterious killer looked back toward the patrolman. He was just passing from view. Relieved, the killer dragged Farrell to the door of the stone building and removed the rusty old padlock, which he had jimmied open earlier. The heavy door squeaked on its hinges as the man pulled Farrell inside.

Working quickly by the moonlight that spilled in through the partly open door, the killer picked up a length of chain and shackled the unconscious lawman to the base of the stone platform in the center of the musty room. Then, using handcuffs stolen long before from the sheriff's office, he attached Farrell's wrists to the chain between his ankles, leaving the federal marshal barely able to move. The killer then stuffed a gag in the lawman's mouth and tied it securely. Satisfied with his work, the man stepped to the doorway and looked out. Another guard was passing, and the man closed the door partway.

Coming to, Farrell began to moan again, rolling his head back and forth, his restricted body already fighting against the chains that held him. Moments later, the marshal's senses cleared, and he opened his eyes to see the dark form standing over him silhouetted by the moonlight. Grunting through the gag, the big lawman pulled against the chain but soon found that he was firmly bound. He lay on his side in a fetal position, with his wrists anchored by the handcuffs to the chain between his ankles. The place was cold, dark, stale, and smelled of decay. At first Farrell could not figure out where he was, but looking past the outline of his abductor, he peered through the doorway and saw the long rows of tombstones gleaming in the moonlight. Looking up, he was able to make out the stone platform that bore the coffin. It was then that he remembered the mausoleum in the center of Lander's cemetery and recalled that it belonged to Buck Durand's long-dead mother.

Cobwebs clung to the lawman's hair and face, and he tried to bring up an elbow to brush them away, but the chain prevented it. The killer stood over Farrell, keeping his face in the shadows, and looked down at the prisoner in silence. Leaning close to the marshal, the killer whispered triumphantly, "You're going to die, Farrell . . . but not yet. First I'm going to bring you someone to keep you company."

With that the killer pivoted and stepped outside. Closing the door, he put the padlock back into place and turned it so that it appeared to be locked. Chuckling to himself, the man skulked through the graveyard and headed into town.

The Reverend Cecil Wright was reading in his study in the church building, where he had been since early evening. Yawning, he laid the book on the desk, removed his spectacles, and rubbed his eyes. He pulled his pocket watch from his vest and checked the time. *Ten-forty,* he told himself. *Time for bed.* Yawning again, he stood up and replaced his spectacles, then blew out the lamp.

Feeling his way to the door, he pulled it open and peered into the sanctuary, lit only by the moonlight streaming through the slender stained-glass windows. As Wright waited a few seconds while his eyes adjusted to the darkness, he told himself that though he had gone against Sheriff Will Iron's suggestion that no one be alone, it was only a few steps from the door of the church to the parsonage.

When he could see more clearly, the preacher pulled the study door shut behind him and started walking toward the center aisle. Just as he passed the pulpit, he halted. Was that a bumping sound? It seemed to come from the back of the sanctuary, near the vestibule, and it crossed his mind that he had foolishly left the door unlocked.

Unable to see much of anything for the deep shadows, Wright told himself he had just imagined the sound and started down the aisle, his footsteps echoing hollowly in the cold, empty building. He passed the last row of pews and moved into the blackness of the vestibule and was almost at the door when he heard a definite rustling sound off to his right. His scalp prickled and his heart beat wildly. Just as his shaking hand reached for the knob, a dark figure leapt at him, driving a knife into his chest. Grunting with pain, he lashed out at his attacker with one hand and fell to the floor.

Feeling for Wright's ankles, the killer gripped them firmly and dragged his victim to a door at one end of the vestibule. He shoved the door open and pulled the minister into a small room directly under the belfry.

Wright was gasping while desperately trying to remove the knife from his chest. Looking at the preacher in the dim light coming through the high window, the killer whispered coldly, "Having a little problem, hypocrite Here, let me help you." Jerking the knife free, he raised high and drove it straight into the preacher's heart. Wrigh died instantly.

The killer dragged the body to the center of the roon and reached for the rope tied to the bell. Pulling on the rope very slowly so as not to jerk the clapper, he made noose, then looped it over Wright's head and let it slowly tighten around the dead man's neck. He then hoisted up the corpse, again careful to do it so slowly that the weigh would not ring the bell.

When the rope had stretched tight, he heard the clapper touch the side of the bell with a dull thud. Wright' feet dangled about four inches from the floor. Ready to go the killer shoved the body hard, causing it to swing back and forth, ringing the bell. Chuckling fiendishly, he made a fast exit.

The town was alerted by the clanging of the bell, and those who had been asleep were now fully awake. When several patrolmen arrived at the church, the bell had stopped ringing, but bloodcurdling screams were coming from within. The guards bolted through the door, guns ready for action, and found Mrs. Wright in the small room below the belfry, holding a lantern and wailing at the top of her lungs.

Momentarily stunned by the hideous sight of their minister hanging by his neck with a knife buried in hi chest, the patrolmen finally collected themselves and quickly took the horrified woman outside. Dozens of people were coming on the run, most of them holding guns and carry ing lanterns. Panic swept through them like a plague when they were told of Wright's murder.

Sheriff Will Iron arrived on the scene, and Dr. John Bristol was called to administer a sedative to Lander' newest widow. Several women accompanied Bristol as he guided the hysterical widow into the parsonage.

Shaking his head, Iron came out of the church build

ing and looked into the fearful faces of the townspeople. He worried that their fear would soon cause them to start shooting at shadows—and each other. After warning them of that very fact, he told them to go home and lock their doors.

Iron turned to town council leader Virgil Orcutt and said, "I need the council members to help me right now. Can you get some of the other men to escort your wives home?"

Orcutt talked to the other councilmen, and soon their wives were returning to their homes accompanied by other women and their husbands. Addressing the members of the council, Iron told them, "Most of the men who are on patrol right now wisely didn't leave their posts at the sound of the bell ringing, no doubt correctly assuming that the closest ones would investigate. I need you men to go in pairs and let those patrolmen know what has happened. And pass this message on for me: If they should locate the killer, they are to try to take him alive if possible. I need to make him confess to killing Errol Durand so Buck Durand can be freed sooner than it will take to clear him through the court."

"We'll take care of it," Orcutt assured him.

"Good. Oh, and one other thing. See if you can locate Marshall Farrell and have him meet me at the sheriff's office in about a half hour. I need to let him know what's happened, too, and discuss more strategy."

By the time Will Iron returned to the sheriff's office, the councilmen were all waiting for him on the boardwalk. Huddling under a streetlamp with their collars turned up against the cold, they informed him that they had been unable to find Tug Farrell, and none of the patrolmen had seen him since early evening.

Fearful that the killer had struck again, Iron told the council they had to begin a search for Farrell immediately. Townsmen were rousted out of bed, and Iron sent them off in teams, bearing torches and lanterns, in search of the missing federal man. Then he hurried into the jail to fill Buck in on what had happened before going back outside to help make a thorough search of the streets of Lander.

When dawn broke, Iron and the townsmen met in front of the sheriff's office. They had not been able to find a trace of Farrell, and a search of every house, outbuilding, and store was begun.

After getting breakfast for Buck Durand, Iron carried it to the jail, where he found the young lawman pacing back and forth in his cell. As the sheriff stepped to the bars with the tray, Buck asked, "What about Marshal Farrell? Has he been found?"

"Not yet," Iron replied, "but I've got almost every man in town searching. The men who were patrolling the perimeter of the town last night insist that nobody left Lander, which means Farrell's got to be somewhere here in town."

Iron slid the tray under the cell door, and his prisoner picked it up and implored, "Sheriff, you've got to let me out of here so I can help search for Farrell."

"I can't do it, Buck," Iron responded, shaking his head. "I know you didn't club Errol, but since he said you did, you've got to be incarcerated until you're cleared. Though most of the people in Lander believe you're innocent, the four ranch hands from the Box D don't, and they would so testify in court. If I let you out before a court has cleared you, I could lose my badge. There's nothing we can do but ride this thing out—but I've given instructions to all the patrolmen that if they encounter the killer, they're to try to take him alive so I can make him confess to clubbing Errol."

Buck sighed and started to speak when a gunshot sounded from somewhere outside. Iron wheeled and rushed to the street and saw people gathering in front of the Lander Feed and Grain Company on Main Street. Sprinting to the store, he shoved his way through the press and entered to find the proprietor, J. C. Dooley, crying and kneeling over his eighteen-year-old employee, who lay with a bullet in the upper left side of his chest.

When the sheriff came in, the stout businessman looked up from the semiconscious youth and moaned remorsefully. Iron knelt beside him and asked, "What happened?"

Sobbing, the proprietor said, "I shot him by mistake, Sheriff! I didn't realize Archie had come in early to do some work in the back room, and—well, like everyone else in town, I've been jittery, so when I heard a noise, I went to investigate. I was carrying my revolver like Marshal Farrell told us to do, and when I opened the door to the room and saw movement, I . . . I fired. Oh, what have I done?"

Looking around, Iron asked one of the patrolmen, "Has someone gone after Dr. Bristol?"

"Yes," the man replied. "One of the other patrolmen was sent for him. We thought it best not to move Archie till Doc got here and looked at him."

The man had no sooner finished speaking when Dr. John Bristol arrived. He made a quick examination of the wound and said he would have to do surgery immediately or the youth would die. Will Iron and several other men carried the youth to the doctor's office, and Jenny Bristol was summoned to assist her father with the surgery. After better than two hours, Bristol entered the waiting room where Archie's parents waited with the proprietor and Will Iron. The doctor quickly relieved their anxiety by stating that the youth would live.

When the parents had gone in to see their son, Bristol remained with Iron in the waiting room. His face etched with worry, the physician remarked sadly, "Sheriff, if that killer isn't caught soon, more of the same thing is going to happen. Everybody is on edge."

"I know," said Iron. "I just wish—"

The outside door burst open and Virgil Orcutt entered, looking weary and upset. "Sheriff," he gasped, "I was told you were here. Sidney Jager's missing! In our search for Marshal Farrell, a couple of us went to the funeral parlor to look through Sid's place, and he's gone!"

"Maybe he just went somewhere."

"I don't think so. His chestnut gelding is in the small corral behind his building along with the team that pulls the hearse, but Sid is nowhere to be found. Before looking for you, I checked all over town. No one has seen him. The patrolmen on horseback insist he hasn't left Lander, but he's disappeared . . . just like Farrell!"

Iron pulled thoughtfully on his gray mustache. Then, shaking his head, he muttered, "I don't know who we're dealing with here. This killer somehow manages to grab people and haul them away right under our noses. It's as though he's invisible and somehow makes *them* invisible, too."

"That's not the way the people are looking at it, Sheriff," remarked Orcutt. "Talk now is that Jager's definitely the killer. They're saying that he's abducted Farrell and for some reason is hiding him in some secret place here in town. They figure he hasn't killed the marshal, or he would have left his body to be easily found, like with all the rest of his victims."

Doc Bristol asked, "Virgil, are people thinking the killer is Sid because he owns the chestnut with four white stockings?"

"That's surely in their minds, Doc," replied Orcutt, nodding, "but they're also asking themselves who would benefit by all these deaths, and the answer keeps coming up the same. Sid is profiting nicely from all these burials—and besides, he's always struck folks as being weird. They're convinced that he is the killer . . . especially now that he can't be found."

Will Iron drew a deep breath and let it out slowly. Rubbing his temples, he stated, "Whether that assumption is correct or not, we're still faced with a mystery. *Where* is Jager—and what has happened to Tug Farrell?"

*   *   *

U.S. Marshal Tug Farrell lay on the cold stone floor of the mausoleum, his body stiff from the cramped position he had been in for so long. He cursed the chains, the gag, the darkness, and the killer. A small crack under the door of the clammy building allowed Farrell to determine that daylight had gone and it was night once more, and an icy wind began whistling through the crack.

The lawman wrestled with the identity of his abductor. The man had spoken in a whisper, obscuring his voice, and he had been careful to keep his face in the shadows. The federal marshal was positive the killer was a local man, well-known by everybody, but he was totally mystified as to his identity.

It had been dark outside for a couple of hours when the padlock suddenly rattled. The door squeaked open, allowing a shaft of moonlight into the gloom, and the vague figure entered. Standing over Farrell, he whispered dryly, "Just wanted to make sure you were still here, Marshal." He chuckled, then added, "I'll bet you're wondering when you're going to die. Well, not until I have your friend Will Iron in here with you!" The killer bent low, keeping his face obscured, and hissed, "I have a special plan for after I chain your friend Iron in here with you. I'm going to kill Buck Durand at the jail and bring his body here. You and Iron will be chained so you can't escape and gagged so no one can hear you. Durand's body will rot, and both of you will have to smell its stench until death comes to your rescue. Nice, though, isn't it? You and Iron can be interred in here with Durand and his mother forever! Newt doesn't come here anymore. He told me. He hasn't opened the door in six years. You're doomed, Farrell!"

The madman laughed fiendishly as he turned to the door, stepped outside, and pulled it shut, rattling the padlock as he put it in place. Listening to the retreating footsteps of the killer, Tug Farrell lay in a cold sweat. *Whoever you are*, thought the marshal, *you are a madman!*

Chapter Thirteen

Jenny Bristol sat on a chair outside Buck Durand's cell, discussing the disappearance of Sid Jager and Tug Farrell. The young brunette told Buck that every building in Lander had been searched again and that the patrolmen on horseback were still insisting that no one had left town. Their ring around Lander had been tight all along, and no one had breached it.

Shaking his head, Buck declared, "This whole thing doesn't make sense, Jenny. Where could Sid have possibly taken the marshal—and why would he hide out, since that in itself points a guilty finger?"

The outside door opened, and footsteps sounded in the office. Jenny stood and sighed. "That'll be Father coming to take me home."

Also rising, Buck reached through the bars, embraced the young brunette, and kissed her tenderly. Jenny took both of his hands in hers and said, "Keep your chin up, darling. Everything is going to be all right. You'll be out of here soon."

The door opened and Dr. John Bristol entered, his coat collar turned up. Rubbing his hands together, he said, "It's getting cold out there. Do you have your gloves with you, Jenny?"

"They're in my pockets," she replied, picking her coat up from the back of the chair on which she had been sitting.

While helping Jenny into her coat, Bristol looked at Buck and said, "It's a dirty shame this had to happen to you, son. We're all hoping the killer's going to be caught real soon and put an end to your having to look at the world through those bars."

Buck smiled grimly. "Thank you for your support, sir."

Her coat buttoned and her gloves on, Jenny said softly, "Good night, Buck. I'll see you tomorrow."

"See you tomorrow," he echoed as the doctor guided her toward the door.

Looking over his shoulder, Bristol repeated, "Good night, Buck."

"Good night, sir," responded the sandy-haired young lawman, watching him go. Noticing something clinging to the back of the physician's coat, Buck was about to call it to Bristol's attention, but the door clicked shut before he could say anything. Shrugging, he sat down on the bunk.

Just before midnight Will Iron entered the cell area. He wanted to check on Buck before he went to the hotel to try to get some sleep, for except for a few short naps, it had been two days since Iron had been to bed. The seasoned lawman informed his prisoner that there still was no sign of Farrell or Jager and admitted ruefully that he was totally mystified.

Telling the young lawman he would see him in the morning, the sheriff returned to the street and had the patrolman who had the jail key lock the door behind him. On the way to the hotel, Iron met another patrolman, to whom he spoke briefly before moving on. Looking forward to getting some rest, Iron was passing a dark passageway between two buildings when a length of two-by-four connected with his head, and he crumpled to the ground. The shadowed figure holding the two-by-four immediately dropped the club and dragged the unconscious lawman stealthily across town.

When he reached the cemetery, the killer hid behind a large tree until a mounted patrolman had passed. Hurrying to the mausoleum, the man removed the padlock and lugged his burden inside. Again working only by the pale moonlight coming through the doorway, the dark figure chained Iron to the stone platform and stuffed a gag in his mouth, just as he had done to the federal marshal. Standing over his new prisoner, he waited for Iron to regain consciousness.

After a few minutes the middle-aged sheriff groaned, and the killer leaned over him and slapped his face with a few stinging blows. Iron came to and began to fight the chains, and the deranged captor chuckled gleefully.

"There's no point in your working so hard, Sheriff, because there isn't any way you're going to get free." Gesturing toward Farrell, he said, "Your friend can attest to that—or he would, if he didn't have that gag stuffed in his mouth."

Iron looked over and saw the marshal for the first time. The two men stared at each other for a brief moment, then the sheriff looked up at the killer, whose face was hidden by shadow.

"Waiting for an explanation, are you? Well, you're chained up inside Lila Durand's mausoleum at the cemetery, where you'll be spending your last days."

Iron groaned through the gag and rattled the chains.

"Don't fret, Sheriff," breathed the killer. "It won't be for too long."

The man suddenly reached around to the back of the platform and produced a lantern. Going to the door, he closed it securely, then struck a match and lit the wick, immediately flooding the small stone building with yellow light. The killer then turned, allowing both lawmen to see

166

his face clearly. Their eyes bulged with recognition, and they tried speaking despite their gags.

The killer sniffed derisively, his eyes glinting insanely. "See there, you're not so smart, are you? If you had the brains you're supposed to have, you'd have stopped me long before now!"

Farrell and Iron strained uselessly against their chains, grunting loudly.

Dousing the lantern, the killer plunged the interior of the mausoleum into pitch darkness. He laughed fiendishly as he shuffled toward the door and said, "Your colleague already knows my plans, but just so *you* know them as well, Sheriff, tomorrow night I will go to the jail and kill Buck Durand, then bring his corpse here. That will give you time to think about the two of you interred with Buck's rotting flesh until you die. But don't worry. Without food and water, a body doesn't last long." Turning the latch on the door, he added heinously, "Sweet dreams. Tomorrow night you can begin your vigil with Buck Durand's body."

The next morning Jenny Bristol was walking down Main Street with Corrie Stenner, who was on her way to the general store in an attempt to get back into the routine of caring for her household. Leaving Corrie near the general store, Jenny crossed the street, heading toward the sheriff's office. Just before she reached the boardwalk she noticed Ford Loker ride across an intersection on his chestnut gelding. Though he had obviously seen her as well, he merely stared blankly until he had passed from view.

Stepping up to the door of the jail, she tried the knob but found it locked. She looked around and saw the man patrolling the area and hurried to him. "Do you have the key to the office, Mike? It's locked."

"Sure do," he replied with a grin, reaching into his pocket. "You want in to see Buck?"

"Yes, I thought I'd visit with him for a while, and then I can take his breakfast tray back to the café for Sheriff Iron—who I'm sure is out concerning himself with more important things."

Scratching the back of his neck, the patrolman said, "I don't think anybody took Buck his breakfast yet, Jenny."

Looking a bit surprised, she asked, "You mean Sheriff Iron hasn't been here?"

"I didn't see him," he replied, unlocking the door and pushing it open. "Of course he has his own key, but I haven't left this block since coming on duty a couple of hours ago, and I'm sure if he'd been here, I'd have seen him."

Puzzled, Jenny entered the office and walked quickly to the cell area, where Buck was waiting at the bars. He had just shaved and smelled of shaving soap.

"Good morning, darling," he said warmly.

Returning his greeting, Jenny kissed him through the bars, then asked, "Has Sheriff Iron brought you breakfast yet?"

"No," replied Buck, "and I'm getting pretty hungry, too. He's never been this late."

"Seems strange to me," she murmured. "Tell you what. I'll run down to the hotel and check on him, and I'll be back shortly."

At the hotel the young brunette followed the desk clerk up the stairs to Will Iron's room. When there was no answer to the clerk's knock, he opened the door and found it empty, with no sign that Iron had been there recently. The clerk told Jenny that he had not seen the lawman come through the lobby the night before and had assumed he was on patrol duty.

Worried, Jenny ran to her father's office to inform him that the sheriff could not be found. Together they rounded up the town council, meeting in front of the jail, and the councilmen were visibly shaken to learn that Iron was now missing as well. The mounted patrolmen were consulted one by one, and they doggedly insisted that the sheriff had to be somewhere in town.

Virgil Orcutt told the group that he had thought long and hard about Farrell's and Jager's strange disappearances, deciding there had to be some sort of secret cellar under one of the barns or sheds in Lander. The others agreed that Orcutt had to be right, and once again a search of the town was ordered.

Dr. Bristol, Jenny, Orcutt, and Mike Hanson went into the jail to talk to Buck. As they filed into the cell area, Buck was standing at the bars, gripping them. "Don't tell me," he said. "Will Iron has disappeared, too."

Bristol sighed and acknowledged, "You're right, Buck. Virgil came up with the idea that there's a secret cellar within the confines of town, and there's another search going on right now."

Jenny took Buck's hand and said, "I'll run over to the café and get you some breakfast. Be right back."

After she had gone, Buck's blue eyes assessed the faces of the three men, and then he pleaded, "You have to let me out so I can do my part to find Farrell and Iron and catch the killer."

Orcutt shook his head. "Buck, there's nothing I'd like more than to have you out there beating the bushes with us, but we could be in deep trouble with the law if we let you out."

Buck punched his palm with frustration. "Look, I realize the bad position it would put you in, but I'm worried that Farrell and Iron are in grave danger—if they're not already dead. The only hope I have that they're still alive is that their bodies haven't been found."

"That's what I'm clinging to as well," the council chairman stated. "I'm sure that with the intensified search now being conducted, the secret hiding place will soon be found."

Jenny returned with Buck's breakfast, telling her father that there were several people lined up at the clinic.

Offering the physician her help, she told Buck that she would return at suppertime with his evening meal.

Hanson and Orcutt also left, planning to join the search, and Buck sat down at the small table in his cell and slowly ate his breakfast.

When he was finished, he stretched out on the cot, pondering the situation. As the hours passed, he grieved over Errol's death and the hatred his father held toward him. Newt Durand's words—*I hope you hang!*—kept echoing through his mind. Then Jenny's sweet words took their place: *When Errol's killer is caught and you're cleared, your father will come to you.*

Buck knew that his father was a proud, stubborn man. He tried to envision Newt Durand coming to him and asking his forgiveness, but the picture would not form. The bullheaded rancher had never done such a thing in his life.

During the afternoon Buck catnapped off and on, and when darkness began to fall, he got to his feet and paced back and forth in the cell. As he repeatedly walked from wall to wall, he told himself there had to be some simple explanation as to where Farrell and Iron were being kept by whoever had captured them. Were they in the hands of Sid Jager? Or was Sid a victim also?

Lighting a lantern as darkness fell, the young lawman continued to pace, running anxious fingers through his sandy hair. Suddenly remembering something he had seen the day before, he stopped in his tracks. Grimacing, he shook his head and said aloud, "No. No, it can't be . . . but it is!" Buck walked to the bars and looked out. Agitated, he muttered, "Jenny's got to let me out when she comes. She's *got* to!"

Time seemed to drag as Buck walked back and forth in the cell. Where was Jenny? She should have been here by now. Calling her name, he told her as if she could hear him, "Jenny, come on! Every minute counts! Hurry, honey! Hurry!"

He stopped pacing abruptly when he heard the outside door open and close. Jenny's recognizable footsteps grew louder as she approached the cell area, and finally the door swung open and she appeared, carrying a tray of hot food. "I'm sorry to be so late, Buck," she said, a bit out of breath. "I was helping Father at the office, and so many people are having nervous problems over this horrible thing, we just closed the office a few minutes ago."

"Never mind that, Jenny," he said intensely, "you've got to let me out immediately!"

She eyed him quizzically and asked, "What are you talking about? You know I can't let you out."

"You have to, honey!" he gasped. "Please! The keys are in the upper right-hand drawer of the desk in the office. Get them, and let me out!"

Clearly puzzled, she shook her head, saying, "Buck, I don't understand."

"I know who the killer is! And I know where Farrell and Iron are being held! Quick, Jenny, let me out! Maybe it's not too late to save their lives!"

Setting the tray on a chair outside the cell, her face filled with bewilderment, Jenny asked, "How can you know all of this?"

"There isn't time to explain! Just hurry and get the keys!"

Hesitating, she asked, "What about the patrolman who let me in? He's right outside the door."

"I'll go out the back door into the alley. You can leave through the front, and he'll never know the difference."

Giving in, Jenny darted to the office. She quickly pulled open the desk drawer and removed the extra set of keys, then hurried back and unlocked the cell door.

Buck dashed out of the cell. Seeing the worry on her face, he assured her, "It'll be all right, honey. And don't worry, you won't get in trouble for this. I guarantee it."

Jenny was on his heels as he made his way to the office. He removed his gun belt from the drawer where

Farrell had put it, strapped it on, and picked up a pair of handcuffs. While he was stuffing the handcuffs in his pocket, his saw his badge in a corner of the drawer and picked it up. Since he was still technically acting sheriff, he would wear the badge and arrest the killer by its authority. As he put on his coat and pinned on the badge he edged to the window and peered out. The patrolman was not in sight. Turning, he gave Jenny a quick hug and headed for the back door, saying over his shoulder, "You go home and keep all of this to yourself until it's over. Don't tell anybody—and I mean *anybody*—that you've let me out. Understand?"

"Yes," Jenny replied. "But please tell me who the killer is!"

Sliding the bolt to unlock the back door, he shook his head and answered, "Later, honey. You'd want to know how I know, which would take too long to explain—and right now every second counts."

With that, Buck Durand was out the back door of the sheriff's office and was gone. Pausing for a moment, Jenny decided to follow him, and she pulled her coat collar up around her ears, hurrying so as not to lose sight of him.

Tug Farrell and Will Iron heard the rattle of the padlock at the mausoleum door and looked at each other, their eyes filled with fearful anticipation. Then the door came open, and the killer entered. Flaring the lantern, he put it on the stone platform beside the coffin and looked at his victims, and his eyes gleamed with a cold, fanatical light. "The time has come, gentlemen!" he announced. "When the town settles in for the night, I'll take out the patrolman on duty by the jail and let myself in. I'll make Buck think I'm going to let him out of the cell, but instead I'll kill him! Soon I will have his body here . . . and the three of you will be locked in here with each other forever!"

Farrell and Iron looked at one another, sweat beading their faces, and grunted through their gags. Their captor was clearly insane, and the madman had them at his mercy.

The three-quarter moon was unsullied by clouds as Buck Durand ran through the dark streets toward the cemetery, unaware that Jenny Bristol was following. The cold air knifed into his lungs as the young lawman gasped for breath in his all-out run. Reaching the cemetery, he threaded his way among the tombstones, slipping periodically on the icy snow covering the ground, and as he approached the mausoleum, he could determine by the crack of yellow light showing at the bottom and along the edge of the door that it was slightly ajar. The light also meant that his quarry was inside.

When he inched closer, he could hear the killer talking softly to someone. Taking a deep breath, Buck drew his gun, cocked it, and steeled himself. Then he raised his foot, kicked the door open, and plunged inside. The killer whirled toward him as the young lawman bellowed, "Hold it right there, Dr. Bristol!"

Chapter Fourteen

Wild-eyed, Dr. John Bristol lashed out with his foot and kicked the gun from Buck Durand's hand. It sailed across the room and hit the wall, discharging. Bristol then lunged for the young lawman, attempting to get a choke hold on his throat.

Buck Durand broke free and slugged the doctor with a powerful punch, then followed it with another. Bristol staggered back, but as Buck reached for his gun, the physician screeched loudly and kicked him. Young Durand stumbled into his mother's coffin, just missing the burning lantern, and grabbed the stone platform to steady himself. The physician went after his adversary again, and they battled fiercely around the mausoleum, even stepping on the two lawmen at times.

The crazed killer was strong and powerful, and his deranged mind seemed to give him the strength of two men. Buck knew he would have to subdue the man quickly before his own strength gave out.

Bristol's steely fingers attempted to close on Buck's throat as the killer shoved him up against the coffin. Thinking fast, Buck spit in the madman's eyes, and the physician blinked against the spittle and yelled, his hands

174

relaxing slightly. Taking advantage of the momentary distraction, the young lawman slipped from Bristol's grip and grabbed his coat collar. Pulling the killer to the floor, he gave a violent jerk on the collar and slammed Bristol's forehead against the edge of the stone platform. The doctor sagged, shaking his head and mumbling incoherently.

Quickly Buck whipped out the handcuffs and rolled the killer onto his belly. As he clamped on the shackles five patrolmen rushed through the door, guns drawn. Peering past them, Jenny Bristol saw her father facedown on the floor with Buck straddling him, snapping the cuffs on his wrists. She then saw the two lawmen in chains and drew in a sharp breath, backing outside and out of sight. Leaning against the wall of the mausoleum for support, she shook her head continually in disbelief and whimpered softly.

Unaware of Jenny's presence, Buck hoisted Bristol to a sitting position with his back against the wall. He then turned and looked at the patrolmen. Virgil Orcutt and big Ken Chitwood were among them. Breathing hard, he announced, "Here's your killer, gentlemen. The good doctor himself."

They gasped collectively, and several of them swore as they looked at Bristol. Working quickly, they removed the gags from the prisoners, then began freeing Farrell and Iron from their chains. The lawmen told of the shock they had experienced when Bristol revealed himself as the killer, and when everyone looked down at him, it was obvious from the look in the physician's eyes that he was demented.

Kneeling beside Bristol, Buck asked, "Will you tell us why you've committed all these horrible murders?"

Almost eagerly, the doctor made his confession. "Let me tell you how it all started," he began in a less-than-steady voice. "Eight years ago, when Jenny was just thirteen, I found out my wife was cheating on me. The day I learned of her betrayal, I had to make a house call before going home, and by the time I arrived home quite late, I was devastated and angry. Jenny was staying all night with a friend, and my older daughter, Lucinda, was supposed to be doing the same with one of her friends. I thought my wife was home alone.

"When I stepped through the door and my wife came to give me a kiss, pretending to love me and that nothing was wrong, I went into a mad frenzy. Grabbing a letter opener, I stabbed her to death, and while standing over her body, I looked up to see Lucinda peering down at me from the top of the stairs. She had watched the whole thing. I tried to talk to her, explain how wicked her mother had been, but her eyes were glazed and it was as if she had not heard me. She completely lost her bearings and slipped into insanity, and her wild rantings led everyone to believe that Lucinda was her mother's killer. The police took her to an asylum for the criminally insane, and the doctors told me her mind was gone and that she would have to be committed there for the rest of her life. Although I would not have allowed my daughter to suffer for me had she been sane, since she would never recover, it provided the perfect opportunity for me. I had initially told the authorities that I didn't know who had murdered my wife, but since it no longer mattered if Lucinda took the blame, I changed my story, telling them I had lied, wanting to protect Lucinda. I told them the truth was that I had come home to find my daughter sitting beside her dead mother with the bloody letter opener in her hand. The police accepted it, agreeing that something had apparently triggered an imbalance in her mind."

The men listened intently as Bristol continued, "When the story came out in the newspapers, I found it hard to face people, so I took Jenny and moved from San Francisco across the bay to Oakland and started another practice. We moved again when word of Jenny's insane sister caught up with us, but after a while things seemed to quiet down. I brought my baby up with love and affection, and I thought that at last happiness and contentment were mine—that is, until my little Jenny started blossoming into a beautiful young woman."

The wildness in Bristol's eyes seemed to intensify as he muttered, "I saw men staring at her. Lechery, that's what it was! It was in their eyes when they looked at her, in their voices when they spoke to her. They wanted to corrupt my innocent little child." Sneering, he declared, "Well, I fixed a couple of them—permanently. But when the police investigating their deaths got a little too close for comfort, I decided it was time to move again, so when I was told about the practice available here, I brought my Jenny to Lander."

His eyes blazing with fury, Bristol snarled, "I thought we would find peace here, but I was wrong. We had been here only a short time when men all over the valley began to leer at my innocent little girl with their filthy eyes. With every day that passed it got worse. I saw it in my office, when she assisted me in treating the male patients; I saw it on the street whenever Jenny and I walked somewhere together. Yes, I saw it even in church! Men and boys looking at my daughter with lust—even that hypocritical preacher. Well, he'll never stare at my little girl again!" He shook his head with disgust, growling, "Males of all types—the respected, the elderly, married or single—all were plotting against me, trying to turn my pure Jenny into a woman just like her mother!"

As Bristol's voice rose, Buck and the others realized that the man was really mad, and he had misconstrued simple friendliness and goodwill for something else. His wife's infidelity had made him murder once; fearing that men intended to harm his daughter by turning her into the same kind of woman as her mother, he began murdering again.

The physician suddenly smiled—a smile of smug satisfaction. "You know what I did, gentlemen? I kept a list of the men in this valley who were trying to lure my little girl into a sordid life. Oh, they pretended they were simply talking to her, but I knew differently. I knew what they *really* wanted."

Swerving his frenzied gaze to Buck, the doctor stated coldly, "At the top of my list were the Durand brothers. I was fully aware of the conflict going on between them as to which one was finally going to defile her. Well, I took care of that drunken sot Errol with the two-by-four. My intention was to kill Errol, hoping that Buck would take the blame." He laughed gleefully. "It worked, didn't it? If it hadn't turned out that way, the blame would simply have gone to the mysterious killer." His mood instantly shifting, he glared at Buck and screamed, "I was going to kill you tonight, you dissolute scum!"

Buck held his tongue.

His rage abruptly spent, Bristol calmly explained that as a doctor, he always had an easy alibi for being away from the office, so following men to kill them was not difficult. And when people believed Swede Andgren was doing the killing, things got even easier. But when Farrell and Iron arrived, the physician grew concerned that they would find him out and arrest him. Neither one had leered at Jenny, but they had to die because they represented a threat to him. So he concocted the scheme whereby the two of them would be entombed with Buck's body.

The doctor grew silent and Buck asked, "What did you do with Sid Jager?"

Bristol laughed. "His body is in one of those coffins stacked up in his back room. You see, my horse developed a sore leg, so I asked Jager if I could borrow the chestnut gelding, telling him I had calls to make out of town. I was actually on my way to kill Ralph Davis when Farrell crossed my trail in the woods, and I panicked and shot at him. But Farrell didn't die and was able to describe the horse his assailant was riding, and things got sticky when word got out and Jager heard it. Fortunately I convinced the undertaker that it was only coincidence that Farrell's attacker had been riding a similar horse."

Pausing for a moment, he continued, "I borrowed the chestnut again, using it to ride out to a ranch to deliver a baby, and afterward I gunned down Ralph Davis—who had never seemed to miss a chance to talk to Jenny when he was in town. The report that Davis's killer also rode a chestnut horse with white stockings made Jager more suspicious than ever, and when I failed to convince him otherwise, I murdered him and put his body in a coffin."

Having finished his confession, the doctor's energy seemed depleted, and he leaned back against the wall and said nothing further.

Suddenly Jenny stepped into the mausoleum, tears running down her face. Hearing her enter, Buck turned and exclaimed, "Jenny! What are you doing here?"

Weeping, she looked at him and murmured, "I've been out there since Virgil and the others came in. I heard it all."

Buck folded her into his arms.

Bristol glared at him with crazed eyes and spewed, "Get your filthy hands off my daughter!"

Jenny clung tightly to Buck and cried, "Buck loves me, Father! You're wrong about him! You were wrong about *all* those men wanting to defile me!"

"That's not so, Jenny!" the doctor countered. "You're just a child! You don't know the wicked ways of men! I killed them to protect you! Everything I did was for you!"

Bursting into sobs, the young woman buried her head against Buck's shoulder. He wrapped his arm around her and led her toward the door, telling the others, "Bring the doctor to the jail, men."

Hurrying through the cold streets of Lander, they reached the sheriff's office and Buck sat Jenny down, trying to comfort her while her father was being locked up in a cell. Tug Farrell and Will Iron remained behind after the guards had left, and when Jenny had calmed down, she looked at the older lawmen and asked softly, "He'll hang, won't he?"

There was dead silence for a few seconds, then Farrell replied softly, "Yes, Miss Jenny."

Her face grim, she turned to Buck. "I want to see Father one last time before I go home. Please let me."

The acting sheriff nodded, and Jenny went into the cellblock, followed by the three lawmen. As they reached Bristol's cell, the killer was standing by a small table that held a pitcher of water, and he was drinking from a tin cup. Gulping what was left in the cup, Bristol set it on the table and approached the bars, his eyes crazed.

Jenny's voice cracked with emotion as she told her father, "Even with all you've done, I can't stand the thought of you going to the gallows."

Bristol laughed humorlessly. Gripping the bars, he exclaimed, "Nobody's hanging me! I've been carrying a heavy dose of strychnine in case things ever turned out like this. I just took it. I'll be dead within minutes."

Jenny's hand went to her mouth as she gasped.

Bristol winced and grabbed his midsection, doubling over with pain, and his face turned gray. Straightening, he reached through the bar toward his daughter, and as he looked at her, his eyes softened a bit and he said quietly, "Good-bye, sweet Jenny. Always . . . always stay as pure as you are. . . ."

The killer laid his head against the bars and jerked in agony. Wanting to spare Jenny, Buck rushed her out to the office, closing the door behind them, while Farrell and Iron remained with Bristol as he died a violent death. When it was over and everyone was in the office, Jenny held tightly to Buck's hands and asked, "How did you know he was the killer?"

"You remember last night when he came to the jail to walk you home?"

"Yes."

"Just as the two of you started out the door, I noticed something clinging to the back of his coat. I started to call out to advise him that something was on his coat, but the door closed too soon. I didn't think any more about it until it suddenly came back to me earlier this evening, and I realized what that clinging stuff was: cobwebs! I remembered getting cobwebs on my clothing each time my father made me go into the mausoleum years ago, and when I realized what was on your father's coat, it all came together. It meant that he had been in the mausoleum . . . and that answered the question of where the marshal and the sheriff were being held. It also meant that your father was the killer."

Horror filled Jenny's eyes as she gasped and exclaimed, "Oh, Buck! My poor sister! Watching Father murder Mother was what drove her out of her mind! She was wrongly accused of killing Mother, and she's locked up in the asylum for something she didn't do!"

Holding her close, Buck assured her, "Don't worry. We'll look into the situation. We can take a trip to San Francisco and visit with Lucinda if you'd like."

"Oh, that would be wonderful, thank you," she replied, managing a slight smile. Then she sighed, her breath catching slightly, and she murmured, "Right now I just want to go home."

By noon the next day everyone in Lander and all over the valley had learned that Dr. John Bristol was the mysterious killer. People were stunned by the news but relieved that the killings were finally ended.

Tug Farrell and Will Iron were at the sheriff's office,

preparing to leave. Iron would ride for Casper to the east, and Farrell would head south for Denver. As they stepped outside with Buck and Jenny, they saw a large crowd of people coming toward them with Virgil Orcutt and the rest of the town council in the lead. The throng drew up and made a large half-circle in the snowy street.

Virgil Orcutt stepped in front of the young couple and said, "Buck, as you know, this council has the authority from the people of Fremont County to appoint an interim sheriff until election time."

The sandy-haired young man nodded and replied, "Yes, sir, I'm aware of that."

"Since the death of Sheriff Stenner, you have been acting sheriff. We all appreciate the way you've handled the job, but as of now, we no longer need an acting sheriff." Extending his hand, he added, "May I have the badge, please?"

Jenny looked at Buck askance, and with puzzlement on his face Buck removed the badge from his coat and handed it to the council chairman.

Orcutt then smiled and said, "We all just held a meeting at the town hall, and it is my duty and privilege to inform you that a vote has been taken by the council and these people—and we unanimously want you as our *permanent* sheriff. Therefore, as council chairman, I want to pin this badge on you as our sheriff until the next election . . . at which time I have no doubt you will be duly elected to remain in office."

Tears filled Jenny's eyes as she looked into the face of the man she loved. Buck nervously adjusted his hat and humbly responded, "Virgil, I deeply appreciate the confidence you and the council and these people have shown in me, but I'm too inexperienced to handle the job. Your sheriff should be a more mature man, someone who's had many years of experience as a lawman. I've only been a deputy for a couple of years."

Will Iron shook his head, a wry grin on his face. "Buck, that's nonsense. I've never seen a man more qualified to wear a sheriff's badge than you. You sent for me because you felt inadequate, but in the end it was you who solved the mystery and brought in the killer, not me. And *you* saved *my* hide."

A rousing cheer went up from the crowd, and the roar of approval became a chant: *"We want Buck! We want Buck! We want Buck!"*

Only when young Durand raised his hands for silence did the chant die out. Smiling, Buck said, "Since Sheriff Iron, whom I admire greatly, has such confidence in me, and because you people want it this way, I'll take the job!"

Another loud cheer went up, echoing off the fronts of the buildings. When the noise had subsided, Virgil Orcutt administered the oath of office to the handsome young lawman and pinned the badge on his chest. There was a round of applause, yet another cheer, and people immediately swarmed around their new sheriff, expressing their thanks for his catching the killer and congratulating him on his new position. Jenny stood by, smiling proudly yet clearly grieving as well.

Tug Farrell and Will Iron said their good-byes to Buck and Jenny and to each other, and rode off in different directions. Virgil Orcutt watched them go, then with the crowd still gathered around, he declared, "Well, folks, now that we have a new sheriff, we also need a new doctor, a new undertaker, and a new preacher."

Buck put an arm around Jenny and told her quietly, "And when we get the new preacher, the new sheriff is going to have a new bride—that is, when you're ready."

Though her whole world had been turned upside down, Jenny managed a smile. "I need you now more than ever, Buck. I'll marry you just as soon as we can find someone to perform the ceremony."

There were ahs from the crowd as Buck and Jenny

enjoyed a long, sweet kiss. The kiss ended and everyone began to scatter, but Buck continued to hold Jenny in a tight embrace.

Jenny looked over Buck's shoulder and suddenly drew away. Pointing with her chin, she murmured, "Buck . . ."

Turning, Buck looked to see what she was indicating and saw a lone rider coming toward them. Then Newt Durand dismounted and stood beside his horse, his eyes glistening with tears.

Jenny released the young sheriff and said softly, "Go on, darling. Go to your father. I'll wait for you here."

THE BADGE: BOOK 21
DEADLOCK
by Bill Reno

After proving himself to the people of Cheyenne Crossing—a full-blooded Cheyenne Indian—was elected town marshal, a position once held by his adoptive father. Now, years later, the marshal's friends and neighbors in that peaceful South Dakota valley are being threatened by Abner Curry, a greedy rancher who wants to own the biggest spread in the region.

After acquiring a ranch through unscrupulous means, Curry and his four sons threaten bodily harm to the owners of adjoining ranches if they won't sell their property for next to nothing and move on. Suspicious, Long Shadow questions the ranchers who are selling out, but those men and their families are so afraid of what the Currys will do to them that they won't admit the truth. Long Shadow, his hands tied for lack of evidence, can only wait and watch closely, all the while keeping the pressure on the Currys.

When the Currys' crimes escalate from extortion to murder, Long Shadow pushes harder to bring them to justice. In the process he makes a mortal enemy of Abner Curry, whose crimes soon hit a lot closer to home. In an effort to free one of his sons from the hangman's noose, Curry kidnaps Long Shadow's young son—and the resulting deadlock promises to end in tragedy and heartache.

Read **DEADLOCK**, on sale Feburary 1991 wherever Bantam paperbacks are sold.